A Low Tea Time in London
英伦下午茶

牛 涛 著
陆道夫 牛 海 译

河南大学出版社
·郑州·

图书在版编目(CIP)数据

英伦下午茶:汉英对照/牛涛著;陆道夫,牛海译.—郑州:河南大学出版社,2020.5
ISBN 978-7-5649-4246-5

Ⅰ.①英… Ⅱ.①牛… ②陆… ③牛… Ⅲ.①诗集-中国-当代-汉、英 Ⅳ.①I227

中国版本图书馆CIP数据核字(2020)第066823号

英伦下午茶

著　者	牛　涛
译　者	陆道夫　牛　海
责任编辑	刘利晓
责任校对	张　珊
封面设计	翟淼淼

出　版	河南大学出版社
地　址	郑州市郑东新区商务外环中华大厦2401号
邮　编	450046　电话:0371-86059701(营销部)
网　址	www.hupress.com
排　版	郑州市今日文教印制有限公司
印　刷	河南新华印刷集团有限公司
版　次	2020年8月第1版
印　次	2020年8月第1次印刷
开　本	787mm×1092mm　1/32　印　张　8
字　数	124千字　　　　　　　定　价　39.00元

版权所有,侵权必究
(本书如有印装质量问题,请与河南大学出版社营销部联系调换)

目 录

Acknowledgements (Niu Tao) ……… (1)

第一部分　往事不如烟
Part One　Sweet Memories of the Past

流年 A Fleeting Time ………… (2)

盛夏的怀念 A Mid-Summer's Memory

………………………………… (4)

童年 My Childhood ……………… (6)

童年的信 A Letter from My Childhood

………………………………… (14)

"爸爸!""Papa!" …………………… (17)

第三号航站楼 Waiting at Terminal

Three ………………………… (20)

玉兰花的初吻 First Kiss from the

Magnolia Flower ……………… (22)

深冬暖阳 Soft Sun in Late-Winter
………………………………（23）
暖夏 A Mild Summer ……………（26）
午后初夏 An Afternoon in Early Summer ……………（29）
雪国公主 A Princess of the Snow Country
………………………………（32）
那年雨季 Those Rainy Days …………（35）
我沿着梦里的长街一路走 Wandering in My Dreams …………（37）
缘分册 If Only We Could Have an Affinity! ……………（40）
旧相册 An Old Photo Album ………（42）
旅行箱 Suitcase …………………（44）
雾都往事 The Old Days in London …（46）
伦敦的下午茶 A Low Tea Time in London ………………（47）
印象英伦 A Dreamland of English Town …………（49）
地球另一端 The Other Side of the Earth ……………（53）
普洱茶的故事 Story of Pu'er Tea …（56）
当年情 Lovely Days in My Heart ……（58）

第二部分　眼前情愫
Part Two　A Love and Sincerity in My Mind

你的眼睛会笑 Your Eyes Can Tell Me a Good Story …………（62）

我的世界开始放晴 My Life Begins To Light Up ……………（64）

我盼望有那么一天 I'm Looking Forward to One Day ………（66）

清澈如你 What a Good Girl You Are! ……………………（69）

你是我一生最美的年华 You Are My All-Life Grace …………（71）

你若是夏花 If You Were Summer Flowers …………………（72）

我能给你的 The Best Thing I Can Do for You ……………（75）

凝望 A Gentle Gaze at You ………（78）

堪比你的美 The Absolute Beauty of You ……………………（80）

一路南下去找你 Down to the South for You Only …………（82）

等一个人 An Expectation from Silly Waiting …………………（84）

我孤独地走在 I Am Walking Alone … (87)
一起走过的四季 The Four Seasons
　　We Spent Together ………… (90)
你留下的 What You've Left ……… (92)
恋之遐想 Mediation on Love ……… (94)
玉兰天使 Angel of Magnolia Flower
　　……………………………… (97)
笑容那样甜 Sweet Smiles ………… (99)
最美的光阴 The Wonderful Time … (102)
孔雀女神 To the Goddess of Peacock
　　……………………………… (104)
花雨仙子 Fairy of Flower Rain ……… (106)
月夜心曲 A Song of Moon Night in My
　　Heart ………………………… (108)
为了你 我温暖地想起 My Warm
　　Memories of You ……………… (111)
暖暖地想起你 My Heart Beats with
　　Yours ………………………… (113)
清朗的午后 A Refreshing Afternoon
　　……………………………… (116)
午后的太阳雨 A Sun Shower in the
　　Afternoon …………………… (119)
书桌 A Small Desk ……………… (122)
长椅上的姑娘 The Girl on the Bench

………………………………………(125)

写诗的夜 A Night for Writing a Poem

………………………………………(127)

你站在海边 You Are Standing by the
Seaside ………………………………(131)

你 听得到吗 Can You Hear Me? … (134)

听说你有心事 Did You Get Anything
on Your Mind? ……………………(136)

稻草人 A Straw Man ………………(140)

花雨纷飞的小径 A Path Covered with
Rainy Flowers ……………………(142)

爱情新纪元 A New Era, a Great
Love …………………………………(144)

第三部分　冥思天地间
Part Three　Mediation on Nature

午后涓涓的时光 Cosy Time in the
Afternoon …………………………(148)

那一条山间小路 The Holzwege Among
Mountain Tracks …………………(150)

随想曲 A Piece of Capriccio ………(152)

花旦 Hua Dan (A Female Role-Play
in Chinese Drama) ………………(154)

飞花 The Flying Flowers …………(156)

太阳雨 A Sun Shower …………… (158)

山水之间 A Landscape in My Mind
………………………………… (160)

我站在风口 I Am Standing in the
Draught ………………… (163)

雨夜旅人 A Traveler on a Rainy Night
………………………………… (166)

煮茶雨夜 Tea-Making on a Rainy Night
………………………………… (169)

品茶 Tea-Tasting ……………… (172)

白马与孤客 A White Horse and a
Lonely Traveler …………… (174)

苦海 An Abyss of Misery ……… (176)

海恋 A Love Song of the Sea ……… (178)

初春 The Dancing Steps of Spring
Season ………………………… (180)

七月天默想 Meditation on Days in
July ……………………………… (182)

深秋明月夜 A Moon-Night in Late
Autumn ………………………… (186)

入冬以后 Late Winter …………… (188)

雪夜 A Snowy Night …………… (190)

雪域 The Snowy Land …………… (192)

林荫道 A Boulevard Lined with Trees

.... (194)

夜 A Night Wears On .... (197)

小园雨夜 A Rainy Night at a Small
　　Garden .... (198)

一半 One Half .... (201)

孤寂 The Solitude of My Life ..... (203)

古镇随笔 Capriccio of a Town ..... (205)

酒吧街 A Bar Street .... (207)

温泉 A Pool of Spring Water ...... (210)

纸船 A Paper Boat .... (212)

月亮船 The Moon Boat .... (214)

今夜 我在吉隆坡 I'm in Kuala Lumpur
　　Tonight .... (217)

年末遐想 One More Year Has Gone
　　............................... (220)

十年 Ten Years Later .... (222)

晚祷 Night Prayer .... (224)

夜城堡 Night Castle .... (227)

东瀛故事 My Stories in Japan ...... (229)

译后记 .... (234)

Acknowledgements

Niu Tao

It has been almost fifteen years since I wrote my first poem, during which I wrote countless poems on various of sad, joyful, nostalgic, and inspirational feelings and emotions. Poems have been, therefore, regarded as my life theme in my heart.

It's been nearly three years since my last collection of poems——*Tears, Splashing Most Beautiful Times* was published in Hong Kong in 2017. Actually during the previous years, I had very bright days and very dark days in my life. Fortunately, I came over smoothly at last.

Even more honored thing is that I have also achieved a kind of success in poems creation. So far, not only have I edited two books of poem periodical, two books of poems collections, but also I've joined the China Writers Association by publishing hundreds of poems, and won several awards in the field. To my great relief, during the past two years, the style of my poems has also changed a little bit, and the verses have become more and more tranquil, more and more soothing. I have been keeping a habit of reading various collections of different poems. In fact, my bookshelf is often full of such kinds of collections. I have four notebooks of great poems, which bring me definitely great happiness.

Whenever I talk about this collection of poems, I am always deeply touched in my heart just because poem is an ethereal art of language. The mother tongue is already very abstract. To translate such an abstract language into English requires a solid foundation of bilingual abilities, not only to remain the original charm, but also to keep it smooth and fluent in English. The difficulties and obstacles to the translation job of Chinese poems into English versions are conceivable. However, I'm so lucky to meet a knowledgeable translator, Mr. Lu Daofu, a professor of English and Chinese Literature in

Guangzhou University, whose translation works are numerous. He has won several awards in the academia field. I can't express my gratitude to Professor Lu in words. To my knowledge, he has devoted to translation of my poems. He gave me constant guidance and encouragement almost every time when I published a new poem. As for his translation of my poems into English, I feel so surprised and honored that such a complicated verse can be translated so smoothly and gracefully to present his extraordinary erudition and bilingual genius. Once more, I'd like very much to express my gratitude to Professor Lu for his great job of English translation.

Here I'd like to thank my twin brother Niu Hai, who participated in partial translation of my poems. We grew up together. He has been taking care of me since we were in the kindergarten. His great encouragement and nice concern always make me feel easy and warm. It is worth mentioning that my brother Niu Hai and I have co-translated a classic of Thomas Hobbes's political philosophy *Leviathan* with Professor Lu in 2019, from which I myself learned too much. With a heart of gratefulness and with the most lively feeling of affection, I always cherish for them the strong emotions and inspirations. I will certainly study harder, work harder and live up to the expectations of my parents, my teachers, and my friends.

Finally, I want to tell readers of this bilingual book: "Let me send you a colorful garland woven with bilingual verses!"

第一部分　往事不如烟

Part One　Sweet Memories of the Past

流　年

谁遗落在草地上
一本未完待续的日记本
谁在旅途中
走丢了一段
旧旧的 泛黄的时光

经过我身边的是
五彩斑斓的流年
夹带着哭与笑
牵着我
走向又一个年头

岁月静好
一如午后温暖安静的时光
当我想起那一串流泪的日子
竟然已经没有一丝的感伤
只留下
不再怕风霜的胸膛

第一部分　往事不如烟
Part One　Sweet Memories of the Past

A Fleeting Time

Who left an unfinished diary
On the grass?
Who lost some old and faded days
On the journey of life?

A fleeting time passed by like an arrow.
I was lucky to see a color of amber.
With tears and laughters,
I stepped into a year of golden bright.

One day of nice makes a year of peace,
Like a quiet afternoon with great warmth.
When I recalled old days with tears——
Not a single trace of sadness
Occured to my mind.
With a strong will without any frost or wind.

盛夏的怀念

你最爱的
那条粉红色丝巾
丝丝缕缕
一环环
都系在了我的青春
等盛夏的藤蔓再爬到你窗口
看看如今
谁又陪着你

暖阳
又折射进那间陈旧的教室
故事
已经落幕了好几年
我怕夏风再升腾起
漫天的蒲公英
把我秘密的心事
散播得人尽皆知

青草上

第一部分 往事不如烟
Part One Sweet Memories of the Past

两只翩翩的蝶

彩色的是你

绿色的是我

替我俩

永远逗留在了

那段明媚的时光里

A Mid-Summer's Memory

A pink scarf you like most,

Strands of thread fasten my youth at best.

Waiting for the mid-summer vines——

Quietly climb to your window.

I am wondering who is right now with you.

Warm sunshine refracts into that old classroom,

Even if the curtain of old story begins to close.

I worry about dandelion's arising——

The summer wind will make me no secrets.

Two butterflies are dancing on the green grass.

The colored one is you, and I am the green.

You and me, two hearts beat as one,

Walk through that bright and beautiful sunshine.

童　年

我看见——

那棵苍翠的榕树

在阳光下慵懒地垂着须

我想起——

那次搬家时走丢的京巴狗

不知在哪里流浪挨饿

我看见——

那只铁锈的闹钟

时针停在多年前的一个下午

我翻开——

那本未读完的格林童话

一片枫叶

第一部分　往事不如烟
Part One　Sweet Memories of the Past

迫不及待地掉落出来

我看见——
那架木造的秋千
一晃就摇过了多少时光
我拨开——
岁月堆积起的层层落叶
依稀可见一串串小脚印

我看见——
柳丝来回划着水面
把小湖撩得直痒痒
我想起——
多年前家里那条金鱼
如果托生在这湖里
它还会认出我吗

我看见——
那个幼小的我
端着豆浆
懒洋洋地走在上学的路上
我听到——
那年春天的课堂上

传来一声声稚嫩的"老师好"

我看见——
那艘作业本折成的纸船
在小溪流上触礁沉没
船上两只首次出航的蚂蚁
拍着溪水大声呼救

我看见——
校园的向日葵笑颜如旧
花坛上写着两个值日生的名字
我想起——
那个胖嘟嘟的同桌小伙伴
总是给课本上的名人画上墨镜或大胡子

我看见——
滑板车孤独地躺在草地上
石凳下
留着不知是谁的一只空水壶
我想起——
那一串串小伙伴的名字
散落在了记忆里的午后光阴

第一部分　往事不如烟
Part One　Sweet Memories of the Past

我看见——

那年和父母一起蹬踩的天鹅船

从湖面上慢悠悠地驶过来

我伸手——

捡起一只水葫芦

画面定格成一片绚烂的夕光

我看见——

从童年伸来的彩虹桥上

缓缓走来

一个儿时的我

我认不出他

他也认不出我

他愣了愣 咧嘴笑了:"大哥哥好!"

我看见——

岁月瞒着所有人

从后巷偷偷溜走

从此杳无音信

直到多年后凝望着这张旧照片

我才知道——

那段无瑕的时光

真的来过

My Childhood

In the large banyan tree of life,
Boughs behind a touch of lazy golden yellow.
The lost Peking-Pak dog occurs to my mind.
I doubt where he is roaming about to starve.

The rusty alarm clock happens to be in my eyes.

第一部分　往事不如烟
Part One　Sweet Memories of the Past

Hands of the clock have just rested——

In an afternoon, since many years ago.

I open an unfinished book of Grimm's fairy tales.

A maple leaf falls down, with itself unable to hold.

The wooden swing happens to be in my eyes.

In a kind of flash, how long did it pass?

The layers of fallen leaves being pushed aside,

I can touch a string of small footprints.

My recall told me that across the water——

Willow branches are scratching back and forth——

To a small lake, a real itch that it gives.

I think of a goldfish at my home

Many many years ago ever since.

Whether it's new life would be in this lake,

No ideas occur into my mind.

A little boy of my pal recalled into my mind,

Lazily walking to school with soya milk at

hand.

A gentle voice came from kids at class——
"Good morning, teacher!"
It melted a cold winter into a warm spring.

I saw a paper boat folded from the exercise book——
Which ran against a small stream to sink.
I saw two ants in the boat:
Clapping the water for help from an outlook.

I saw sunflowers on campus——
With their usual smiling faces.
Two students were on duty that day.
Their names were written on the flower terrace.
I still remembered that chubby desk-mate.
He enjoyed drawing on textbook celebrities,
To put them on sunglasses and long beards.

I saw the scooter lying alone on the meadow,
While his empty kettle on stone bench below.
I recalled names of my little pals.

第一部分　往事不如烟
Part One　Sweet Memories of the Past

The cosy time scattered all of my sweet memories.

That year I saw a swan boat with my parents——
Coming over quietly from the lake surface.
I stretched out to pick up a water hyacinth.
The picture was then framed into a gorgeous sunset.

I found myself back to childhood of a Rainbow Bridge,
Greeting me softly like an old pal for many a year.
He could not figure me out.
Neither could I ——
He was stunned, and grinned, "How are you, my big brother?"

I know that everyone lagged behind times,
Sneaking away from the backlane,
Hearing no words or messages between lines.
It wasn't until years later that——

I learned it from this old photo, too.
I did have wonderful time in my childhood.

童年的信

咚咚拨浪鼓
蓝白相间的小皮球
还有
攒了一个夏天的动漫贴纸
粘了满满一厚本

浓绿茂盛的梧桐树
垂下万千缕温暖的阳光
幼年的我蹲在地上
小心翼翼地玩蚂蚁

幼儿园放学的钟声
是童年最曼妙的音乐
书本收起来 乐器放起来
奔向在门口等候的父母
一路上
叽叽喳喳地说着这一天的趣事

第一部分　往事不如烟
Part One　Sweet Memories of the Past

我好像是误乘了一辆时光机

岁月还没等我反应过来

便沧桑了容颜

煮尽了时光

等到午后放学时间

我又漫步在

这条归家的林荫道

捡起了一片梧桐树叶

伤怀的情感

沿着树叶的纹路静静延伸

我知道

那是

童年寄来的一封匿名信

A Letter from My Childhood

Tok, Tok, Tok, a rattle drum is singing,
Blue and white, a rubber ball is rolling,
I collected cartoon stickers in the whole summer.
They covered all of my books with colors.

Deep green and lush phoenix trees,
Flapped down numerous strands of warm sunshine.
Along with a juvenile, I was squatting on the ground,
Playing with ants with a big care.

The bell ringing after school in kindergarten,
That was the most pleasant music of childhood.
Put away books and music instruments,
Rushed towards my parents waiting at the door,

第一部分　往事不如烟
Part One　Sweet Memories of the Past

Jabbered fun of the day all the way home.

As it were on a time machine by mistake, how could it be?

Yet before I know something about the secrets,

Time is already past, and youth is lost.

After school in an afternoon,

Here I was again, wandering on this avenue home.

I picked up a phoenix tree leaf.

Sadness extended quietly along its veins.

I know for sure that——

An anonymous letter from my childhood.

(Translated by Niu Hai)

"爸　爸!"

我看着你静默的脸庞
等岁月的皱纹慢慢爬上来
等到很久以后的一天两鬓斑白
你还是 高高挺立着

依然是一个坚强的男人

把时光的指针往回转百万圈
咱们再去海滩捡贝壳
逆着夕阳柔光的身影 一大一小
咱们再去沿着泥泞的山路往上爬
你一定想再把我架在肩膀上
因为 就是因为
那么 那么快
我就壮得让你再也抱不动了

我不管
就算是下辈子
你也要牵着我的手
一起走一辈子
倘若我们失散了
我跋山涉水 走遍地球
也要找到你
然后像我们从前一样
小小的我与大大的你
飞奔过去 再喊一声洪亮的
"爸爸!"

第一部分　往事不如烟

Part One　Sweet Memories of the Past

"Papa!"

I'm staring at your peaceful face.
Although wrinkles are climbing up slowly,
And temples are getting into grey,
You are still standing as tall before,
A man who is so tough in my heart.

Turning back the pointer of time to a million turns,
Let's go to the beach for picking up shells.
The figures, a tall and a small,
Are against soft light of the setting sun.
Let's climb up to the muddy mountain road again.
You must be eager to put me on your shoulders as before.
Because, just because…
I've grown up so fast,
That you can't carry me any more at last.

Whatever it will be, even in after life.
You must take my hand,
Go together for a lifetime.
If we both were lost,
I would walk all over the world,
Trying hard to find your steps.
Like what we used to be,
Small as me, while big as you,
I'll rush over and brightly shout out——
"Papa!".

(Translated by Niu Hai)

第三号航站楼

第三号航站楼
弥漫香气的咖啡店
我用借来的纸笔
草草记下这一趟旅行的欢欣

第三号航站楼
夕阳折射进我的眼眸

第一部分　往事不如烟
Part One　Sweet Memories of the Past

金光灿烂的大理石地面
倒映出无数的过客 行色匆匆

第三号航站楼
夜已经越来越深
这趟晚点的无期限的航班啊
恰似我生命中迟迟还没出现的她

Waiting at Terminal Three

At Terminal Three,
I smelled an aroma-filled café,
With borrowed paper and pen,
I jotted a joy of another land.

At Terminal Three,
Into my eyes, the setting sunlight reflected into room here and there.
The brilliant golden marble floor,
Greeted each passers-by in a hurry through the door.

At Terminal Three,

The night was getting darker before me.

I was just waiting for this uncertain delayed flight,

Which reminded me of her endless absence in my life alike.

(Translated by Niu Hai)

玉兰花的初吻

风

在摇晃满树的繁花

一朵玉兰花

飘落下来

拂过我脸颊 轻轻一吻

我的心刹那间被感动

因为那是

玉兰花的初吻

第一部分　往事不如烟

Part One　Sweet Memories of the Past

First Kiss from the Magnolia Flower

The blossom flowers
Dangled above the tree in the wind.
One magnolia flower
Was buried into my mind——
With a tender kiss on my cheek,
By a momentary melting into my heart.
It was just a first kiss
From the white magnolia flower.

深冬暖阳

在午后醒来
窗外的阳光
透过梧桐树林
斑驳地折射到我房间

桌上的咖啡
温热的浓情在蒸发

我写的那一首长诗
还搁笔在第一段

听一张收藏了好久的旧唱片
冥想着
与一首首老歌有关的回忆
歌里唱的故事
美满得让人向往
伤怀的情绪
蔓延着像窗外的藤蔓

走出小楼
沿着梧桐树林的小道
向着深冬的更深处
慢慢地走 慢慢地走

故事缺了谁
如今也不遗憾
我有洒遍树林的暖阳做个伴

Soft Sun in Late-Winter

I woke up in the afternoon,
To find sunshine outside the window.
The mottled sunshine——
Reflects into my room alone,
Through Chinese parasol trees line by line.

On the table, there is a cup of hot coffee.
A passion is going to evaporate.
The long poem I haven't finished yet——
Rests on the very first paragraph.

I am listening to an old record of my favorite,
Meditating on some sweet memories in old songs.
The happy story in the old song——
Makes me yearn for things on and on.
A sentimental mood is spreading over——
Like lines of vines outside the window.
So I am going out of this small building,

Walking along a path at this forest of Chinese parasol,

Towards a very deep winter,

A deeper winter step by step slowly.

Well, nobody could be a hero of that old story,

I have no regrets in my old memory,

Because I've got a soft sunshine——

That sprinkles all over the woods with my good companion.

暖　夏

慵懒的梦
交织着许多凌乱的往事
从午后迷糊地醒来
屋檐下就只我一个人
热气蒸腾的心房里
隐约又出现了那个她

那年盛夏

第一部分　往事不如烟
Part One　Sweet Memories of the Past

那场热恋

被高温晒到了沸点

我推开门痴望你

披一身艳阳的光影

映入我眼眸温暖的笑颜

流年流转到这一夏

那段故事早已经全剧终

我抬头望望骄阳绚烂绽放

至少它见证了我们的相遇

等到下一年

又经过

春的翠

夏的暖

秋的凄

冬的凉

我还要暖暖地记起

那一年盛夏

你暖暖的笑颜

至今还温暖着我

A Mild Summer

A lazy dream——
Mingled with many past events in a big mess.
In the afternoon I woke up in a daze,
Sitting alone under the eaves.
And with time passing by,
Somehow she loomed up in my warm heart.

That mid-summer,
That passionate love,
Was both heading over to the top.
I opened the door to stare at you,
Wearing a bright sunny shadow,
Your sweet smile was reflected in my eyes.

But, but…oh…oh…
What a pity for those flying times.
The old story turned out to be an end of great warmth.
The story ended with a great hope!

I looked up at the brilliant sunshine,

For our first meeting witness at least.

We had experienced season after season——

From the green spring, the hot summer,

The bleak, desolate autumn,

Until the white winter with freezing coldness.

I will always remember that lovely summer with you,

A mid-summer that year to be apart,

You've left your gentle sweet smiles in my deep heart.

午后初夏

风拂过初夏

花园里的每一片绿叶

载着每一寸阳光

仿佛在静止的时光里

扮演一个沉默的配角

我静坐在这座小花园里

从我年少

就爱呆坐在这里

听风 听雨 听落花声

幻想着 盼望着 长大的岁月

而我如今

已经成熟

却怎么

那么想回去

那些青葱的时光

我呆坐在这里

心里泛起

一声唤我的乳名

一声放学的欢笑

还有

所有在这里想过的心事

An Afternoon in Early Summer

A gust of wind from early summer——

Is now gently touching my cheek.

Each piece of the green leaves in the small garden,

Reflects upon every inch of golden sunshine.

In such a time at a standstill,

The wind cannot but play a supporting role.

In this beautiful pocket garden, I am sitting at ease.

I've been sitting here ever since I was very young.

I was used to different wind and rain of its voice.

I was happy to see the flower petals falling to the ground.

I had fantasy about how life would be with my growing-ups.

But nowadays,

Although it is the period in which——

My mind attains a kind of maturity,

I am still cherishing those years of my own story.

I enjoy sitting here with peace.

Something touches my heart with a sweet sense.

A whisper of my pet name comes to me so close.

Not only do I hear a peal of merry laughter after school,

But also I see many worries or troubles through.

雪国公主

片片雪 片片霜花
终于载不动我沉重的怀念
一刹那崩溃便飘洒成灾

你那里
也开始下雪了吗
我看见雪花沾染着你的长发
冻红的脸颊
风雪中仍甜的温暖的一抹笑
宛如这雪国里的公主

这一场雪
一场虚构的童话

第一部分　往事不如烟
Part One　Sweet Memories of the Past

手捧的雪花瞬间被融化

踩下的足印慢慢被掩盖

那个我为你造的憨厚雪人

肯定活不到明早日出

我每日扫雪

清理门前归家的小路

你若回来

能不能记起

来过的我的家

A Princess of the Snow Country

Snowflakes and frost flowers in fragment——

Bearing my heavy nostalgia at that moment.

I happen to have a nervous breakdown at once,

Dissolving into tears of yearning, falling ceaselessly on my face.

Is it also snowing at your place over there?

I can't just help wondering.

I see snowflakes mixing with your long hair.
I feel your frozen red cheeks——
Wearing a kind of sweet smile with warmth——
Like a snowy country princess.

It is the heaviest snowfall.
It is a winter fairy-tale romance.
Snowflakes at my hand melt at once.
Heavy snow covers up the footprints.
And I am sure that——
The simple snowman I made for you
Won't be able to survive until tomorrow.

Every day I have to sweep away the snow
For cleaning up a path to the front door.
If you are back home, I would like to know——
Whether or not you could have my home recalled.

那年雨季

浸染了花香的你的唇
在我那年的雨季里
留一个粉粉的印
在日记本
泛黄的光阴里
还能依稀可见
你穿白裙转身的背影

原来我流离了半生
有一个清纯的姑娘
还一直站在
我那段久久以前的青春里

多年后的一个梦乡里
我又骑着那辆旧单车
你坐在我身后
我们哼着歌
一路往林荫道的深处
啦啦啦 啦啦啦

一点悲伤也没有

一点遗憾也不留

Those Rainy Days

A slight breeze rose from your lips,

Awaiting the heavy scent of flowers to fly to me,

Left me with a pink kiss for my rainy days.

Our youth seemed to have gone with the wind in a wink.

And your figure in white dress could be still faintly seen.

For most of my life, I had to wander from place to place.

I was so lucky to meet such a pretty and innocent girl as you——

Who had been waiting for me within my youth still.

That was an old story long long time ago.

第一部分　往事不如烟
Part One　Sweet Memories of the Past

Years later, I had a dream of my hometown.
I rode again that old bicycle on——
While you sat on the bike behind.
We sang happily as we rode to the end of avenue.
La la la, la la la,
You tapped your feet, hummed merry tunes,
Without any grief in waves,
Not a single regret we had to continue.

我沿着梦里的长街一路走

我沿着梦里的长街一路走
雾里仿佛是她无助张望的目光
一整夜
纷纷乱乱的低语声
一路上
洋洋洒洒的残红雨
扰乱我惊慌的愁绪
彻夜无法安眠

我沿着梦里的长街一路走

黑暗中
紧锁的城门尘封起一段往事
长路上
凌乱交错的明月光
长路上
一袭白纱的她的影
撩动我满心的惆怅
彻夜泪眼蒙眬

我沿着梦里的长街一路走
满街飘飞的柳絮纵身飞上夜空
这一夜
烛火跳动的红灯笼
这一夜
无法停歇的脚步声
把我逼到长街的尽头
让我惊醒
在冷雨纷纷的夜半

Wandering in My Dreams

I was wandering in my endless dreams.
The mist seemed to witness her helpless gaze.

Whispers burst out all night around.

The pouring red rain fell to the ground,

From which a feeling of sadness arose.

Throughout the night, I had to be a man of sleepless.

I was wandering in my endless dreams.

A period of past events was sealed up without any loss,

In a very deep darkness.

The moonlight seemed to be at a big mess.

All the way around,

Her shadow seemed to be in white gauze,

Leaving behind drizzling melancholy in my eyes.

I was wandering in my endless dreams.

The catkins were flying all over the streets,

To jump up into the night sky.

The red lantern with candle flame moved up and down.

The footsteps kept going on and on,

Driving me to the end of this street,

I came to wake up in the pouring cold rain at midnight.

缘 分 册

惆怅
堆积在我心房
半空中结了蜘蛛网
蒙尘的往事
被风吹成了灰

日出到迟暮
初识到分离
是一圈一圈
永不停歇的轮回

假如
我当初没有说再见
假如
你我没有失散在十字路口
假如
缘分册上

第一部分　往事不如烟
Part One　Sweet Memories of the Past

我们的名字靠在一起
那今天 或许

If Only We Could Have an Affinity!

A spasm of sadness piled up in my heart.
The cobweb had been netting in the air.
The past events had——
Turned into a thick layer of dust present.

From a sunrise to a sunset,
From the first meeting to our final leaving,
All seemed to alternate rounds of rounds,
Like a kind of Samsara of Heaven,
Never-never-resting.

If only I did not say goodbye to you,
If only we could have a kind of affinity,
It would be a wonderful today, or maybe a promising tomorrow——
Another kind of destiny might follow——
Forever between me and you.

旧 相 册

无意中
再翻开我们那一本
搁在窗台上的旧相册
你熟悉的容颜
一刹那
击中我的心

花海里
温存的记忆
树林间
透出阳光的甜蜜
还有
咖啡屋里你一杯 我一杯
浓香的香草拿铁

我狠狠心
把相册合上
锁进记忆的柜子里
任它在里面无言地哭

第一部分　往事不如烟
Part One　Sweet Memories of the Past

从此以后
绝口不提
直到一天
我们彼此全都忘记

An Old Photo Album

I happened to re-open an old photo album of you and me,
　　I was leaning against the sunny window.
　　I was so familiar with your sweet faces.
　　You beat my heart in a moment with a blow.

　　The memory of tenderness in the flower sea,
　　The sweetness of the sun through the trees,
　　And in a coffee house,
　　You and me, one cup after another,
　　We were enjoying fragrant vanilla latte.

　　I closed my album without any hesitation,
　　Locked it into a cabinet of sweet memory,
　　Let it sober in a silence.

Since then, we shall never mention it again.

Until one day, both of us shall be each other's stranger.

旅 行 箱

我提着

一整箱的记忆与眼泪

满满的 沉沉的

我不知道

能不能再塞进去

第一部分　往事不如烟

Part One　Sweet Memories of the Past

一张已泛黄的你的旧照片

我拎起
一整箱的春光与秋色
鲜艳而悲凉
我不知道
能不能再塞进去
一颗藏在回忆里的星辰

Suitcase

Memories and tears,
Occupy all my suitcase.
Too heavy, and too many,
Sorry, I am not sure by myself——
Whether or not, where or how,
There is another place for an old photo of yours.

Sunshine of spring, and bright colors of golden autumn,
Reflecting upon my suitcase.

With a little melancholy sometimes,
Sorry, I do not know——
Whether or not, where or how,
You could plug a star in,
With bitter memories of buried and hidden.

雾都往事

仿佛是依稀在眼前
那座泰晤士河的桥上
你着蓝色百褶裙走来
浓甜一笑
暖透伦敦暮色里的天与地

岁月蔓延过经年后
往事早已搁浅在泰晤士河滩上
风干 蒙尘 退化
雾散后
河的两岸
一半是愁怨 一半是怀念

第一部分 往事不如烟
Part One Sweet Memories of the Past

The Old Days in London

As if I could still see you,
On the bridge of the Thames.
You came to me in a blue pleated skirt,
With a merry sweet smile,
Warming up the whole London in twilight.

Years have passed by.
History has already been stranded on the Thames beach,
Dried, dusted, and degraded.
The fog is off, at the two sides of the river.
Half is melancholy, half is nostalgia.

伦敦的下午茶

伦敦的下午茶
夕阳斜映进百叶窗
安静又温暖

我现在

缺一杯

可以融化悲伤的拿铁咖啡

还缺一个

能够倾诉心声的

中国姑娘

第一部分　往事不如烟
Part One   Sweet Memories of the Past

A Low Tea Time in London

A low tea time in London,
Sunset slants into the blinds,
Idling with a charming peace.
At this moment,
I am in need of, and eager to get——
A cup of latte coffee to melt my sadness.
A Chinese girl flashes into my minds.
To her, I am definitely at a big loss——
How to pour my heart out?
How to let her know my heart?

印象英伦

慢慢地 慢慢地走进
这一座如梦似幻的英伦小镇
十二月凉凉的雨
淋在我棕色的大衣上

也有过几次露水般的缘分
也有过几段彷徨惆怅的岁月
雨水中的老旧火车站
进进出出着离愁或欢喜

再也没有了
再也没有了她的音讯
无法偶遇
也无从寻觅
她是不是冬夜的那个梦中人

这条老街走到了尽头
身边掠过一张张异国的面孔
我身上的英镑
不够我买一杯拿铁暖暖身子

在河的对岸
是雨雾中的教堂
安详的古建筑
敲响了晚钟
我的晚祷
是想再见她一面

第一部分 往事不如烟

Part One Sweet Memories of the Past

轻轻地

轻轻地告别

这一座飘着冷雨的英伦小镇

来日的朝朝暮暮 夏雨秋风

再也与你无关

再见了

再见 也许只在梦乡

A Dreamland of English Town

Gently, softly, slow down your steps,

Wandering in this dreamland of English town.

In December, the cold rain falls down.

I have to put my brown down-jacket on.

A kind of dew-like fate appears,

The melancholy of one day and a year loss.

An old train station was found in the rain,

Carrying various sadness and gladness out or in.

Not a single word from her could be heard.

Her voice turns to be silence in my ear.

I just can't happen to meet her somewhere.

Isn't she a dreamer of winter night?

An exotic face like mine turns up at the end of this old street.

But I don't have any pounds to get a cup of Coffee Latte.

On the opposite bank of the river,

A church stands in the fog and rain.

The night clock rings against a serene ancient building.

I pray at night for my last look at her again.

Gently, softly, with mild and sweet words,

I say goodbye to the twilight of this English town in a cold rain.

No matter it is summer rain or autumn wind,

No matter it is a bright day or a dark night,

What leaves you alone in my heart,

With a kind of dream, I have to say goodbye.

第一部分 往事不如烟
Part One Sweet Memories of the Past

地球另一端

穿过校园碧绿的河流

摇晃着一整夜

无眠的愁绪

我摘一颗最亮的星辰

挂在书包上

做成闪闪吊坠

古老时钟的指针

转了一圈又一圈

离归家的日子

还远得望不见

但我的心不凄凉 不孤单

就在举目天涯的某个地方

有人为我日夜牵挂

图书馆的灯盏

明亮一整夜

我抿一口香草咖啡

接着读这本陈旧的爱情小说

等到天际蒙蒙亮

我要去看

最远的楼台

望一望

从北半球跋涉到此的朝阳

它此日

又为我捎来

一句来自故土暖暖的

暖暖的口信

The Other Side of the Earth

A clean river runs through the campus——
Shaking away sleepless sadness all night.
I pick up one of the brightest stars——
To hang it on my schoolbag in a twinkling pendulum.

Round and round, the ancient clock turns its pointer.
I have to count my fingers for my day back home,
Because I often have a lonely heart,
Because somewhere in the world far away,
Someone often cares about me day and night.

All the night, the library is very bright.
A cup of vanilla coffee I prefer to take,
An old love story I'd like to read.

I read and wait——

Until the horizon changes into a little white.

I step on to the farthest terrace for a look out——

Enjoying a sunrise from the northern hemisphere away so far.

It's coming to me again today,

Carrying me with a message away from my hometown so far——

A warm message for my great delight.

普洱茶的故事

熟悉的普洱茶香

透过纸窗

熏醉了窗外街灯下的梧桐

我捡起一片梧桐叶

上面写满了春夏秋冬

无数个琐碎的故事

一股莫名的情绪

顺着梧桐叶的纹路

慢慢延伸

用许多个日夜的悲喜
沏一壶浓浓普洱
灌醉我心头

等夜到深处
等我饮尽普洱
我把这些年的故事
全都讲给你听
长长的
旧旧的
远远的
淡淡的

Story of Pu'er Tea

Familiar fragrance of Pu'er tea,
Spreading through the paper window,
Intoxicated the phoenix tree under the streetlight.
I picked up a phoenix tree leaf,
Loaded with plain stories of each season.
An inexplicable mood of mine,

Slowly expanded along the veins of the leaf.

Sorrows and joys kept company day and night,
A pot of thick Pu'er, is thus made
To intoxicate my mind.

Until when it was late at night,
Until when I took all Pu'er tea from cup,
I would post all of my old stories
Into your heart,
No matter it was long, or short,
No matter it was old, or new.

(Translated by Niu Hai)

当 年 情

我已不是当年的我
你也不是当年
让我心动的那个你
擦肩而过后

第一部分　往事不如烟
Part One　Sweet Memories of the Past

缘分荒芜了好多年
你也有了你的他
我也继续孤身流浪
只有在泛黄的日记本里
才能找回
当年
为你流的泪
为你暖暖的笑
还有
闪烁着星光流彩的书信里
一行行浓情
调制成的甜蜜告白句

Lovely Days in My Heart

I am not what I used to be.
You are not what you used to be that year,
Who made my heart beat.
Among seas of the crowded,
You and I brushed.
How time flies!
What a fate of big ridicule!

Year after year, one after another,
You've got your own prince.
I've never kept my own loneliness apart,
Letting it stored in my old diary.
Can I find back our sweetness of tears——
Together with a warm laughter in the letters?
Like littering stars in the sky
Confessing to you with happy sweet words in my heart?

第二部分 眼前情愫

Part Two A Love and Sincerity in My Mind

你的眼睛会笑

你的眼睛会笑
一汪湖水般的眉眼
漾着四季的艳丽
那是
我爱的唯美风景

你的眼睛会笑
玉兰花般清纯的眼眸
一眨一眨
仿佛要对我说话
那是
我最爱的闪亮目光

第二部分 眼前情愫
Part Two A Love and Sincerity in My Mind

恬淡

Your Eyes Can Tell Me a Good Story

You have charming eyes,
With a blue water of eyebrow,
Seeing through gorgeous seasons of the year.
That's the beautiful scenery in my diary.

Your eyes are charming and bright,
As pretty and innocent as magnolia flower,
Blinking an eye for a love confessing.
That's why I can feel sparks of your wisdom shining.

我的世界开始放晴

我的世界开始放晴
艳阳暖透了雨
着白色衣裙的她
在山坡上起舞
一回眸的温柔
像一朵玉兰绽放在晴空下

我的世界开始放晴
南风吹干了泪
裹粉色披肩的她走进我的花园
一转身的妩媚
像倾城的百花撒遍我的世界

My Life Begins To Light Up

There is a ray of sunshine in my life.
I love to recall such sunny hours on summer day.

The bright sun cleans up the rainy sky.

She is dancing on the hillside in her white skirt.

A hundred charms reveal from her glancing back and smiling,

Like a magnolia flower blossoming under the sunshine.

There is a ray of sunshine in my life.

The wind from the South dries up my bitter tears.

She is wearing a pink shawl over her white dress,

To walk into my small garden.

A graceful look on her face upon her turning round——

Like seas of flowers blooming in profusion.

我盼望有那么一天

我盼望有那么一天
我可以骑着单车载着你
沿着稻田旁的小路
一路走到日落
你紧紧地靠着我 靠着我
沿路都是爱情最美的风景

我盼望有那么一天
我可以和你坐着热气球
慢慢往天空升起
融进洁白的云海
远望斑斓的彩霞
你紧紧地牵着我的手
爱情在一万米的高空如烟花绽放

我盼望有那么一天
穿越竹林 越过小石桥
到我们的小屋
摊开宣纸

悬笔写一个你的名字
挑灯看明月
泻影在湖面
一圈圈涟漪
全是你我爱过的轨迹

I'm Looking Forward to One Day

I'm looking forward to one day——
When I am riding a bicycle carrying you——
To a stretch of green paddy fields along the muddy trail.
We are walking on and on until a golden sundown.
You are leaning against my back,
And I am backing your happiness.
The most beautiful scenery of love——
Covers all the way along.

I'm looking forward to one day——
When I take a balloon with you across the countryside,

Rising slowly and slowly to the blue sky.

Both of us melt into cotton-white sea of clouds.

Looking up at rosy clouds from afar.

You and me, hands in hands without any loose.

Our love is bursting at a height of 10,000 meters.

I can lift up the world with one hand if you're holding the other.

I'm looking forward to one day——

When we can walk across a bamboo grove and a stone bridge,

Coming quietly to our own cottage.

I am picking up brushes and rice paper,

To write out your name in one smooth motion.

Looking up at the bright moon over the lake through the red lantern,

The ripples of various sizes and shapes——

Have witnessed what our love miracle is.

清澈如你

清澈如你
微红的酒窝泛起一串涟漪

温柔如你
微微上扬的嘴角勾住了甜蜜时光

可爱如你
圆圆的脸颊是我最爱的轮廓

美丽如你
一转身在琴声中翩翩起舞

难忘如你
你的音容印刻在我余生的岁月里
永不苍老

What a Good Girl You Are!

You are a girl of innocence with simplicity.
I can find a ripple in your reddish dimple.

You are a girl of tenderness with passion and warmth.
I can recall those happy times setting on your lips.

You are a lovely girl with a good virtue.
I can feel your round cheek full of catchy tunes.

You are a beautiful girl with an artistic temperament.
How amazing to see you fluttering and dancing to music of elegance.

You are a girl who is very amiable and unforgettable.

And your sweet smiles will be engraved on me like the pure white marble.

你是我一生最美的年华

有你的日子
是我曾经最美的记忆
忘了在哪个十字路口
失散了彼此
迷路的青春从此冷雨纷飞
过了许多年
遇过许多人后
我还要骄傲地说
你是我一生最美的年华

You Are My All-Life Grace

Sweet days with you,
A decent memory in my heart,
Which cross shall we lose for a new?

The lost youth passes away with the cold rains.
Though years have gone,
Though many a person come across among,
I shall sing you a beautiful song——
My heart is always filled up with your grace,
With no sign and sadness of my lips!

你若是夏花

你若是夏花
只开这一季
又何苦惹我痴狂
流连醉于花海绚烂

你若是驿站
只留过客一晚
又何苦夜半奏一曲筝韵幽幽
扰我无心读书卷
醉心你芳音

你若是渡船

第二部分　眼前情愫
Part Two　A Love and Sincerity in My Mind

只载我过这程波澜
又何苦诉你漂泊半生的苦泪
令我心托付在这孤舟

你若只是经过
经过我惯了孤单的人生
又何苦　又何必
回眸一抹浅笑
从此见你
只在夜夜梦乡

If You Were Summer Flowers

If you were summer flowers——
Blossoming only in this season,
Why got me annoyed with such a fool for you?
In your gorgeous flowers, why let me fully indulge?

If you were a courier station,
Where a passer-by could only stay for one evening,

Why did you bother me with tune tinkled from Chinese Zither?

And your melody at midnight distracted me from books reading.

If you were a ferryboat,

Just carrying me for one time to sail through the great billow,

Why did you bother me with your nomadic bitter tears?

How could I entrust this ferryboat with my confidence?

If you were just a passer-by,

If you'd like to experience what my lonely life was,

Why did you bother me with your gentle smiles?

Because never could you have such imagination——

That I am eager to dream of you every lonely night.

第二部分　眼前情愫
Part Two　A Love and Sincerity in My Mind

我能给你的

我一贫如洗

满怀是悲伤与凄迷

我能给你的

只能是最璀璨的诗行

诗里撒满

澄澈的星光

诗里悬着
想念你的泪光

我一贫如洗
半生流离在茫茫人海
我能给你的
只能是最浪漫的诗行
香水百合
开在每一句的开头
碧水涟漪
荡漾在每一句的结尾

我一贫如洗
但我用最勇敢的心
恋着你
我能给你的
只能是最绚烂的诗行
生生世世
年年月月
字字句句
仍然是写不完的
你的美

第二部分　眼前情愫
Part Two　A Love and Sincerity in My Mind

The Best Thing I Can Do for You

I am as poor as a church mouse.

But I am gently licking the baffle inner pain and chill.

So what I can do for you is——

The only most bright lines of my poems.

My poems are a blaze with starlight.

My poems are filled up with glistening tears of your shinning light.

I am as poor as a church mouse.

I am also a restless wanderer on the earth.

So what I can do for you is——

The only most romantic lines of my poems.

Each line begins with a blossom of the Perfume Lily.

Each line ends with blue ripples gleaming.

I am as poor as a church mouse.

But I love you like a man of great courage.

So what I can do for you is——

The only most gorgeous lines of my poems.

Can anyone keep this promise generation after generation?

But your sweet days of deep feeling with a great love in my mind,

And your absolute beauty can never be written out.

凝 望

我痴痴凝望

幻想着花海中的你

是醉或是心痛到极致

你是那样遥遥不可及

我孤单凝望

窗外撑红雨伞的你

梦一般清纯的姑娘

转眼

消失在茫茫雨水中

第二部分　眼前情愫

Part Two　A Love and Sincerity in My Mind

我醉心凝望
你站在那座桥上
向我挥手
我就这样
任你身影铺满我天地
一生悲欢喜乐
都因你而起

A Gentle Gaze at You

I don't know why I'm still hanging on,

Or I'm still waiting for you all around,

Until I see you stand out from a sea of flowers in a vision.

I have my countless share of heartaches or drunken sense,

Deriding the crowd between you and I,

Our distance and love turns into a kind of flight.

I'm staring at you all by myself.

You are holding an umbrella outside the

window,
Appeared to be as pure as a lily in my soul.
But even by scanning through in the rain,
I can't find your swift leave.

I have my own infatuations to gaze at you.
I've caught sight of your waving to me by the bridge.
My life has been fully occupied with your shadow.
All of my joys and sorrows will be recorded in a white page.
Nobody can have this secret but I myself really know.

堪比你的美

还能有谁
堪比你的美
你飘舞的白裙
舞醉了一身的彩蝶
你纯净的眼眸

第二部分　眼前情愫
Part Two　A Love and Sincerity in My Mind

含泪时多么让人心疼
你温柔的唇语
绵绵这一季的秋雨
我把红尘踏遍
却找不到
还能有谁
堪比你的美

The Absolute Beauty of You

I wonder who else it could be
To surpass your absolute beauty?
You are dancing in white skirt, light and graceful,
Overshadowing the colorful butterflies.
Your eyes are so pure and clean——
That I hate to see your sweet tears of pain.
How much of your tender whisper could it be
To melt down this continuous autumn rain?
I have seen through the immortal vanity,
But I've found nobody else could be matched
To surpass your absolute beauty.

一路南下去找你

一路南下去找你
江南小巷里
寻觅你撑纸伞穿旗袍的秀影

一路南下去找你
乘小舟穿过万丈烟雨
你或许就在烟水尽头的阁楼里

一路南下去找你
策马狂奔过红尘千里
原来你就在南国 等了我好几世

Down to the South for You Only

I am going down to the South——
All the way just for your appearance.
I've zigzagged down a labyrinth of alleys,
Trying hard to find your slender figure,

In fashioned Chi-pao and with a traditional paper umbrella.

I am going down to the South——
All the way just for your appearance.
I've shot the rapids in a canoe among the misty rain.
I guess you might be in the attic,
Watching thick mist and drizzle in the morning.

I am going down to the South——
All the way just for your appearance.
I am galloping down mountains and hills across,
Into a spiritual world of Shangri-La.
Oh, My God! How happy I am to realize——
That you've been waiting for me in the South,
Ages and ages with me so near.

等一个人

原来
等一个人
可以这样的美好
在街灯下徘徊
反复排练见面时的台词
胸口隐隐地跳动
加上一丝美妙的心痛
幻想在这一街飞花中
与她可以紧紧相拥
或许等某天某地
为她穿上纯白色的婚纱

我在路灯的昏黄中傻笑
灵魂快要出窍 像个痴呆
连街边的白猫
也望着我发愣
幻想着她 穿着蓝色百褶裙
从粉红花雨中走来
就这样等她吧 细数一分一秒

第二部分　眼前情愫

原来等一个人
可以这样的幸福

An Expectation from Silly Waiting

I've never thought it a beautiful thing to wait silly for someone,

A situation of my wandering under the streetlight.

I am going over those lines of the first appointment,

With a faint beating of my chest,

With a feeling of my heartache.

I am lost in reverie that——

We can embrace each other with a merry tight,

All around this flying flowers of the street.

I have even fantasized about our romantic wedding,

For somewhere on some day,

She is best for her wedding dress in pure white.

Whenever I fancy about this romantic situation,

Under a dim light of the street, I can't just help giggling,

Feeling like a fool with body and mind apart.

A white cat at the corner of the street,

Seems to laugh at me as if I am in a trance.

I am fantasizing about her sudden approaching,

To me in her beautiful blue-pleated skirt from the pink flowers of rain.

Well, I am waiting for her at ease with my fingers crossed.

Never have I thought it a beautiful thing to wait silly for someone like this.

我孤独地走在

我孤独地走在

这个寂寥的梦境里

梦里

有缭绕的淡雾

梦里

有凄惶的野草

我却盼不到

那个梦一般的姑娘

我忧伤地走在

这条苍凉的小河边

河边

有高高的芦苇丛

河边

有炊烟袅袅的人家

我却遇不到

那个穿白色连衣裙的淳朴的姑娘

我疲倦地走在

这个华丽的礼堂里

屋里

有璀璨耀眼的吊灯

屋里

有一闪一闪的蜡烛

我却找不到

那个披一身婚纱宛如仙女的姑娘

我彷徨地走在

这座幽静的古城里

城里

有万盏高高挂着的灯笼

城里

有一排排古色古香的小楼

我却等不到

那个前世就有约

今生还未来的姑娘

第二部分　眼前情愫

Part Two　A Love and Sincerity in My Mind

I Am Walking Alone

I'm walking alone,
In my solitary dream,
Where there is haunting mist,
Where there are desolate weeds.
But I can't see you,
A dream-like fancy girl as you.

I'm walking sadly,
Along this bleak rivulet,
Where there are tall reeds,
Where there are houses with smoke,
Curling up from kitchen chimneys.
But I can't come across you,
You are my simple girl in a white dress.

I'm walking languorously,
Into this ornate auditorium,
Where there are bright drop-lights,
Where there are glowing candles,

But I can't find you,
My fairy-like girl in a wedding dress.

I'm walking uncertainly,
In this peaceful ancient small city,
Where there are highly hung lanterns,
Where there are old-fashioned buildings.
But I can't wait till your appearance,
You are my yet-to-come girl
With an appointment in the future.

一起走过的四季

似花果淌着蜜
似明月在浅笑
等我攀上了枝头
摘一朵绚烂夏花
不及你一半的甜美

甜甜的心
甜甜的你
回眸一笑

第二部分　眼前情愫
Part Two　A Love and Sincerity in My Mind

倾倒了日月
我捧一束黄玫瑰
摆在你怀里
我摘一朵玉兰花
插在你发髻

我今生最美的风景
是牵着你
一起走过的四季

The Four Seasons We Spent Together

The nectar is gathered from flowers and fruits.
The crescent moon smiles in doubt at its round face.
As soon as I climb up the branch,
I pick up a spectacular summer flower,
Which is not so good as your beautiful smile.

Your sweet smile makes me full of vitality.
No sooner do you glance back and smile——

Than you can reveal a hundred charms over the moon.
I hold a bunch of yellow roses,
Putting them in your soft arms.
I pick up a magnolia flower,
Putting it in your fragrant bun.

The most beautiful scenery in my life is:
You and me, hand in hand,
From the cradle to the grave
Two hearts beat as one in the colorful four seasons.
We make our own beautiful promises.

你留下的

你留下的青梅酒
让我醉了这一夜
你隔着烟雨
眺望我的动情目光
让我倾心这一世
你留下

第二部分　眼前情愫
Part Two　A Love and Sincerity in My Mind

未填完的诗词
使我百思
冥想不出佳句
你留下的
没有结局的这一段情
使我抱憾这一生

What You've Left

The plum wine you left——

Got me drunk tonight.

Your beautiful eyes——

Behind the misty rain,

Kept my heart beating with pleasing.

The poems——

You had not finished yet.

Although it was hard to write,

Nothing good to match your beautiful eyes.

I know that never would I forget,

The endless love you have left.

恋之遐想

倦了 倦了

稿纸上的诗句

停在第六行

她的印象太模糊了

她的身姿太绰约了

寥寥几笔

再也描绘不出

当初见她的惊艳

可我还是
想为她作一首诗
当作我们相遇过的凭证
那条林荫道
至少还残留着她的脚印
那轮红日
至少目睹过我们的遇见

也许
真的太难忘
她一转身的妩媚和闪亮
可惜
我只是
一个一贫如洗的诗人
诗章上的甜蜜字句
在现实中沉默又无力
容我安静地
冥想她的美
把她倾城一笑回眸
深深地写进
今夜的梦乡里

Mediation on Love

A kind of languor,
The intolerable ennui of my writing.
The stanza of my poem,
Resting only on the sixth line.
Because of her vague image,
Because of her faint figure,
Not a single word is able to picture,
Her grace of beauty at my first sight.

Even it is the case,
I should have written a story of us between.
A poem for her never stops in my pen,
Recalling us upon our magic first meeting.
Her footprints somehow were left——
On that path filled up with color green.
And the red sunshine witnessed our greetings in the fresh morning.

Perhaps, or maybe,

It is really too impressive to forget,

Her image with shining charm——

Upon her beautiful turning around.

But nobody knows how poor I am,

I am only a shabby poor poet,

Though sweet words are all through with my pen,

These words are silent or soft in reality.

These words allow me to have a peaceful mediation:

On her unique beauty in my heart,

On her unforgettable smiles in my mind,

All has been rooted in my dream,

Deeply, deeply in the silent evening.

玉兰天使

玉兰花开

绽放两瓣纯白的笑颜

我好像

又忆起

你素面朝天

在暖阳下
微微扬起的嘴角

那是
清流洗涤过的目光
那是
玫瑰红晕染过的脸庞
一丝一毫
也不曾被这浊世沾染
多么像天使安详

Angel of Magnolia Flower

The magnolia flower is blossoming.

The two petals break into a pure white grin.

I used to recall your beautiful face without make-up.

Your sweet smile on your lips can be seen.

A clear water creek can be mirrored in your bright eyes.

A red rose flush suffuses your fragile face,

Like many flowers coming out of the mud without a stain.

Whoever knows, how much could it be?

Because you are a great angel of my future plan!

笑容那样甜

我想用花瓣折一只粉蝶
偷偷放进你的首饰盒
当你孤单时
粉蝶便扑翅围着你盘旋
纷乱着你柔柔的目光

阳光斜映在百叶窗
折射走入我一个午后的梦乡
如若你还是孤单一人
我就在梦里的后花园里等你

时光逆流着忧伤与欢欣
你的笑像明月一样
可爱地挂在天边

倘若你就此离我而去
我想我
就再也遇不到像你一样
笑容那样甜的女子

Sweet Smiles

A pink-colored butterfly was folded with petals for you.

I stuffed it into your jewelry box without any notice.

When you are one by yourself,

The butterfly will flap its wings to circle you around,

And your pretty tender eyes thus be shined upon.

The sun is slanting against a shuttered window.

The refracted light leads my day-dream to grow.

If you were still a single,

I would prefer to stay in the back garden of your golden dream,
Waiting quietly and patiently for you, and for you.

How time flies!
Against the current of joie and sadness.
The bright moon decorates your sweet smiles,
And your smiles cast light into my dream.
If you want to leave me alone here and now,
I am thinking, and I have to suppose——
That such a sweet girl like you will never come up on earth!

最美的光阴

甜得像蜜一般的你的笑
美得像谜一样的你的故事
你在月光下回转身姿
碎花连衣裙舞动着落红

我与你相对站着
我与你隔着一帘烟雨
却怎么遥远得
像离你有千山万水

柔得像丝绸一样的你的目光
暖得像红日一样的你的掌心
我们站在青春最亮的地方
跳一支舞
惊艳了最美的光阴

The Wonderful Time

Your sweet smiles are as lovely as honey.

Your secret stories are as beautiful as riddles.

I watch your turning around in the moonlight.

I watch your dancing with fallen flowers in a floral dress.

We are standing on opposite sides, looking at each other.

In spite of our distance by a curtain of misty rain,

It seems that only a step lies between you and me,

But we might fly over the mountains and seas.

You have your gentle eyes as soft as silk.

You have your warm palm as hot as the sun.

We are dancing with our brightest vigorous youth,

And our wonderful time shall last forever long on and on.

孔雀女神

一朵芙蓉出水
身上挂着湖底青鱼的眼泪
我在阁楼上静听琵琶曲
冥想你的美

孔雀绚烂开屏
绽放开一个绝美的梦
你的身姿在月光下翩翩起舞
为我献上一场华丽的孔雀舞

明月映照你清纯的面庞
嫣然一笑陶醉了众生
我饱蘸一笔浓墨
描天地绘彩霞
却始终难画出
我心里最美的你

To the Goddess of Peacock

A Lotus rose from the water.
Herring tears were hanging on her figure.
With all my ears at ease,
I was listening to Pipa music at the attic,
To taste your beauty of mind peace.

The peacock displayed its splashes color of wing.
A beautiful dream was thus arising.
Silhouetted against the moonlight,
Stood your figure of great grace,
Favored me with a colourful Peacock Dance.

Bright moon on your happy face——
You and me, enjoyed together, looking far to the horizon.
When you flashed your swift smiles,
Crowds of people arrived at a sudden of silence.

Though I was able to finish an excellent paint of:
The Heaven and the Earth.
Yet, nobody knew——
How hard to have a portrait of you.
Because your beauty is beyond all description of my soul.

花雨仙子

百合花幻化的仙子
舞动在我梦畔
花瓣洁白
似初恋的
纯如一张
倾城容颜略施的粉黛

一路林荫落红成雨
纷纷花瓣打在我身上
仿佛是
她给我的千百个甜吻

等初秋的月牙上梢

等今夜梦乡的剧情

华丽开幕

我闭上眼睛

就能看到

花雨中的梦

花雨中的你

Fairy of Flower Rain

A fairy of flower, was dancing in my dream.

Her petals were as pure as my first love.

Her face was fascinating with light make-up.

Shade all the way, blossom fell like rain.

Petals were falling on my shoulders,

Just like the sweet kisses from her to me.

When the moon crescent of early fall rises,

When the dream of tonight gorgeously begins,

With my eyes closed,

I can find that,

Dream and you are all in the flower rain.

(Translated by Niu Hai)

月夜心曲

幽凉的月光

顺着柳枝滴落

点染开

碧水上澄澈又细碎的涟漪

凌空而下的一滴泪

落在你手中

静静浸润

当年我放在你掌心的约定

第二部分　眼前情愫
Part Two　A Love and Sincerity in My Mind

还温存在
你每一道掌纹中

今夜
趁着月明
我共你羽化成蝶
扑翅闯开阵阵迷雾
倘若暗云又遮蔽了月明
我便衔千万绪柳丝
为你造一个甜梦

曾流转了
几世风雪的命途
你一直都活在我的诗里
等到清霜染了双鬓
我还为你执笔
因你是我一生
永不枯竭的诗情

A Song of Moon Night in My Heart

Willow branches are fluttering gracefully,

In the coolness of moonlight tonight.

Ripples over the clear water,

Folded into little rays of golden brightness.

A drop of tear,

Is falling to your hands from the high air,

Like spring rain, soaking into our appointments.

I used to put tears on your palm that year——

Turning into a warm affection in your palm prints for a share.

By the moonlight tonight,

You and me, from pupae to butterfly,

Flapped our wings to break through the flurries of mist.

If the moon were covered by the dark clouds again,

I would rather pick more willow branches fine green——

To set up a bright nest for your sweet dreams.

Although hardships of destiny were handed

down from generation to generation.

You have been always my poems inspiration.

I know that one day even I am going to get older with gray hair.

I am all ready to write poems with all of my passion,

Because you are the immortal greatest poetry of my life,

Like a harbor in the tempest,

A river in a time of dryness,

And eyes in a moon of blindness.

为了你 我温暖地想起

为了你
我温暖地想起
那颗流星
擦亮了我的全世界
我在繁星下许愿
但愿有一天
与你在夜空中重逢

为了我
请你别忘记
我推开心扉
躲进你的全世界
但愿
你的世界
能容纳孤单的我
遮风又挡雨

My Warm Memories of You

I can feel your love of warmth,
Sweet memories of you——
Never have I forgotten in my heart.
I spotted a shooting star to raise me up bright.
I enjoyed making my own wish under the stars at night.
I wish I would have a reunion with you in the Milky Way some day.

For my sake, could you please——

Keep our memory in our noble mind?

I wish to open all my heart,

Resting quietly on your side.

If only you would save room for my lonely heart!

How fantastic to share a sweet safe bosom for our love shelter!

暖暖地想起你

每当这样的清晨

我便会轻轻地想起你

你朱红的唇印

吻红了天上的彩霞

你明亮的眸子

好像枝叶上晶莹的露珠

每当这样地想起你

我都会情难自禁地掩面偷笑

每当这样的午后

我便会暖暖地想起你

你甜甜的浅笑

暖透了
整个秋末的寒冷
你温柔的眼神
是我心中流过的暖流
每当这样地想起你
我都会偷偷躲在书房
为你写一首情诗

每当这样的夜里
我便会柔柔地想起你
你飘起的裙摆
舞乱了
一地萧瑟的枫叶
你静默的唇语
似乎诉说着
你离开我的缘由
每当这样地想起你
我都会捧着你的照片
流下一滴暖暖的泪水

My Heart Beats with Yours

The first rays of sunlight rise slowly in the morning,

Your softness and tenderness makes me refreshing.

Your vermilion lip prints,

Kissing over the sky through roseate clouds.

Your glorious bright eyes,

Like bright dew drops on the tree leaves.

Every moment when I have you on my mind,

My great happiness can't be buried behind.

When the sun reaches its height at noon,

I can't help thinking of your charming warmth.

Your sweet smile——

Warming up the cold and chilly late-autumn.

Your gentle eyes——

Lighting up a warm current to water a dry heart of mine.

Every moment when I have you on my mind,

I am eager to write a poem for you about my story inside.

When the sun sets down at early night,

I can't help thinking of you to be very quite.

Your dancing skirt in the cloud——

Is like wind-tumbled maple leaves on the ground.

Your wordless lips——

Seem to send me secrets of our parting.

Every moment when I think of you,

I can't help feeling upon your photos again and again.

And I have to admit that——

Maturity is not the aging heart but smiles with tears in our eyes.

清朗的午后

天空澄碧

白云

往梦的国度飘

我想化作一只风筝

挣脱了线

飞往

白云生处的仙境

闭上眼安静地听

时光流逝的声音

青春淌过的声音

时间是一把细沙

那么那么快地流逝干净

还好

这午后的时光

流淌得这么慢

让我静下心来回忆

这一年的故事

我会好好保存着

命运

赠我的欢笑和眼泪

A Refreshing Afternoon

Cotton-white clouds hang over the blue sky.
I want to become a flying kite,
Without a roll of strings——
Flying to a fairy land of great depth.
With a peaceful mind,
With my eyes closed,
I——, I——
Listen to the voices of:
How time flies!
How youth flows!

As time turns out to be a handful of fine sand,
Leaking out as quickly as rain drops.
Well, thank God for blessing,
At this lazy noon,
Time flies not that fast.
So I might be lost deep in mediation:
On my old stories the year before.
I should well cherish to a destiny,

Away my tears and smiles can be easily cast.

午后的太阳雨

午后
从梦里醒来
屋檐外
一场太阳雨
人间被洗涤得好清澈
漫漫青草地上
每一株草
托着一滴泪

我心里的你
又似一场太阳雨
一半阳光的温暖
一半冷雨的忧伤
缠缠绵绵
交织着美丽

雨恋着红日
红日为雨意乱情迷

奈何乌云散尽后

夜幕来临时

阳光也被黑夜瓦解

雨水也被轻轻风干

多么像

时至今日的你和我

A Sun Shower in the Afternoon

In the afternoon,

I woke up from my dream.

A sun shower is dripping from the eaves.

The amazing clarity of the world brings me rays of warmth.

At the boundless expanse of green grass,

Every blade of green grass,

Is glistening with tear-drops everywhere.

You are in my heart,

Like a sun shower.

One half is the brilliant sunshine.

The other half is a melancholy where the cold

rain rests.

A haunting melody between you and me,

Tangles together the greatness of our love beauty.

A red sun with a cold rain,

Stands not a single minute from apart.

A red sun brings her ecstatic happiness.

But what a pity!

That dark clouds have dissipated,

And the evening progresses,

The sunshine has sunk to be very dark.

A rain has been dried up so quickly,

That how much it looks like,

A kind of love so far so great,

Between you and me,

As we glide through the dark,

And glow under the stars,

We'll drift to island of wonder that gleams.

书　桌

我爱伏在我的小书桌上
橘黄的小台灯映照着面庞
一纸潦草的心事和回忆
被折进信封里封藏起来

我爱伏在我的小书桌上
书桌与木书架
紧紧靠着　相依为命
我翻开一本泛黄的散文集
找一个去年引我流泪的小故事

我爱伏在我的小书桌上
一杯清茶的雾气
开出了一朵美丽的梦想
我把梦一口喝尽

我爱伏在我的小书桌上
微风吹进屋子
翻乱了诗章

那是一本我想送给她
却始终没送出去的书

我爱伏在我的小书桌上
书架上
藏着一本本故事和传奇
我翻开一本浪漫的小说
一头扑进了
这个缠绵悱恻的故事

A Small Desk

I love sitting by a small desk at my study.
The orange-lit lamp shines upon my face.
And my small discretion and memories,
Are folded into an envelope for another day.

I love sitting by a small desk at my study.
The small desk and wooden bookshelf have similar destiny.
I date back to an old book of essays——
To read a short story,
Which touched me into big tear.

I love sitting by a small desk at my study.
A vapour from the green tea,
Makes my beautiful dreams start to blossom.
I can't wait to swallow up all of the dreams.

I love sitting by a small desk at my study.
The poem book is ruffled by the gentle

breeze.

That was her gift I wanted to give.

But it still remains on my bookshelf so far.

I love sitting by a small desk at my study.

The bookshelf is occupied by books of legends and a good story.

I open a book of good romance:

Indulged in such a sensitive love of great grace.

长椅上的姑娘

你坐在长椅上的背影
美若一幅油画
纯白的连衣裙上
落下几瓣粉红的樱花

花不说话
静静依偎在你怀里
那便是我都嫉妒的曼妙
你是谁呢

长椅上的姑娘
你是否也像我
心事重重 忧伤满怀
明早你会发现
长椅上
我赠你的粉色诗集
第一首诗
就叫作《长椅上的姑娘》

The Girl on the Bench

I see your fine figure on the bench,
As beautiful as an oil painting.
The pink cherry blossom petals are falling,
Onto your silk shirt-dress in virginal white.

The flower doesn't have any words to tell me,
Snuggling up quietly in your arms.
I envy this miracle of your great beauty.
And if it weren't you, then who could it be?
Hey, the girl on the bench,
Can't you be very similar to me?

Will you be also laden with a kind of anxiety,

Or with a mixture of sadness and hope?

I am not sure whether you've caught sight of anything,

On the bench the next morning.

It is a pink book of my poem collection,

Of which the first poem is entitled with——

The Girl on the Bench.

写诗的夜

窗外

夜风摇晃着梧桐

月影斑驳地投射在窗台

我的组诗写到一半

灵感便枯竭了

要不要

刻意再干枯地续下去

唱机里

传来怀旧的音乐

一段段伤感的歌词

押韵得漂亮

一首歌记载着

我十年来的记忆

百听不厌的是

悠扬的旋律

悲伤得恰到好处

我的白猫

趴在毯子上睡着了

墙上的标本蝴蝶

鲜艳却无法飞翔

时光安静得

像沙漏里的沙

一点一点流干净

然后 一切重新来过

关掉灯光

抱着布娃娃坐在窗台上

窗外的湖水泛着波光

柳枝蘸着清澈的涟漪

在水面来回地划

我定睛一看

她在续写完

第二部分　眼前情愫
Part Two　A Love and Sincerity in My Mind

我停笔在一半的诗歌

A Night for Writing a Poem

Outside the window,

Sycamore trees are waving in the breeze.

Moonlight shadow is dappling the windowsill.

I have finished only half of my sequence poems,

Because my inspiration has been dried up to death.

Shall I deliberately continue or not to write?

Nostalgic music comes from the record player at the moment.

Paragraphs of sentimental lyrics,

Are beautiful in a nice rhythm.

A song records my ten-year memories,

Never do I get tired of listening to these stories.

The rising and falling melody——

Is just sadly to the point.

A white cat falls into sleep on the blanket.
The specimen butterfly on the wall,
It is colorful but unable to fly any more.
Time is as quiet as sand in the hour glass,
Running away little by little,
And then all is over, and over.

I stand up to turn off the light,
Sitting on the windowsill.
The lake outside the window,
Flooded with glistening light of waves.
Willow beaches dipping in clear ripples,
Sweep on the water back and forth.
After my closer look,
I come to know that——
She has kept writing something on and on,
Until half of my poems have been already done.

你站在海边

你站在海边
白纱裙
随风摇摆
暗蓝的天空下
你的剪影
美得让人惊叹

你站在海边
风拂动你的长发
但风和我一样却猜不透
你此刻的心事

你站在海边
捡起了一个斑驳的贝壳
握在手心
像握着我们的约定

你站在海边
遥远的天际

晕红的云霞

好像你的脸颊

椰风把你抱紧

惹得我嫉妒

你站在海边

海潮声中

你的眸光闪烁

我牵起你的手

走入碧蓝的海水

走进美妙的年华

You Are Standing by the Seaside

You are standing,

By the seaside at ease.

And your white skirt can be seen,

Moving freely back and forth.

A pretty silhouette of yours,

Sets off a beautiful arc through the azure sky.

And your beauty turns out to be amazing.

第二部分 眼前情愫
Part Two A Love and Sincerity in My Mind

You are standing,

By the seaside at ease.

A gentle breeze is brushing against your long hair.

I'm standing against the wind to have no idea:

What's on your mind at that right moment?

You are standing,

By the seaside at ease.

To a piece of mottled shell you are drawn.

You pick it up and hold it at your fingertips.

As if our appointments are within your plan.

By the seashore, you are standing,

Looking out to a very far horizon.

The rosy clouds are gorgeous,

Bending over to your red cheek for a kiss.

A gentle breeze from the coconut tree,

Holds you tightly in its arms.

For all of this, I admire but not envy too much.

You are standing by the beach.

The tides come and go as they will.
The twinkle in her eyes is so clean
That hand in hand I will be with you till the end.
You are my azure blue Aegean Sea.
Between the salty water and the sea strand,
Then you'll be a true love of mine,
Always finding new beauty in our life melody.

你 听得到吗

落日敲青山
敲碎了一颗等待的心
那一种心碎的感觉
弥漫在黄昏的空气里
余味 是两行泪的涩
你听得到吗

风雨揉碎了落花
一生柔情全都赴了流水
宛若这颗心
碎成了一地紫水晶

第二部分　眼前情愫

子夜 窗外有一个人在呜咽
你 能听得到吗

Can You Hear Me?

A spectacular sunset is knocking the green mountain,

Together with my broken-heart.

And I treat it as a kind of painful feeling.

There's a mood of gloom and despondency in the air.

Two lines of bitter tears are filled with a nasty after-taste.

Oh, you——you——, and you——

Can you hear me? Can you feel it by ear?

Petals have been quickly blown away by wind and rain.

A deep feeling of my great tenderness is just in vain.

Like this deep broken heart,

A pane of amethyst has cracked,

Splintering into pieces to the ground.
At this lonely midnight,
A man is sobbing outside the window.
Oh, you——you——, and you——
Can you hear me as it will?

听说你有心事

听说你有心事——
我焦急地等候在你归家的路上
路上是一地初秋的雨
一路昏黄的灯

听说你有心事——
我一遍遍拨着熟悉的电话
在微凉的夜里来回徘徊
"对不起,您拨打的电话无人接听"

听说你有心事——
我呆坐在秋林旁的小湖边
对着繁星一遍遍默念
"你在哪里?"

听说你有心事——
我等候在你屋子的窗台下
想分担你的忧伤
擦干你的泪
让你靠靠我的肩

听说你有心事——
我把思念绑在白鸽的腿上
让它代我去找你
白鸽呀 求求你捎回她的音讯

Did You Get Anything on Your Mind?

I heard that you were bothered by something.

On your way back home, how anxious I was waiting!

The early autumn rain fell endlessly to the ground,

With the faint light of the roads on.

I heard that you were bothered by something.

So I was dialing that phone number again and again.

Though I was wandering back and forth on the chilly night,

A familiar voice burst into my heart:

"Sorry, the call you dialed is not answered."

I heard that you were bothered by something.

So I just sat in the autumn forest by the lake,

Looking up to the stars, whispering again and again.

"Where are you?" "I promise to wait for you."

I heard that you were bothered by something.
So I was standing below the ledge, waiting for you in silence.
Sharing all my joys to lessen your grief,
Wiping away all your bitter tears,
I want to put your head on my shoulder, arms in arms.

I heard that you were bothered by something.
If only I could ask a white pigeon
To take my messages to her.
"Pigeon, pigeon, white pigeon,
Could you please let her feel my passion?"

稻草人

我是田边的一个稻草人
衣衫褴褛 满面尘土
面对着远山 成天笑呵呵
飞鸟落在我肩上
它是我最好的朋友

我从来没有告诉过别人
我心里暗恋着一个人
她住在山边的小房子
她喜欢穿着黄色连衣裙
静静坐在小湖边

我的嘴巴说不了话
我的腿走不出一步
我只能这样
只能这样偷偷地望着她

有一天夜里
满天都是星光

第二部分　眼前情愫
Part Two　A Love and Sincerity in My Mind

我做了一个梦

我变成了一个英俊的青年

捧着一束玫瑰

敲开她的门

梦里朦胧的光影里

她是那么的那么的美

A Straw Man

I'm a straw man standing in the field,

With ragged clothes and a dusty face.

The high mountain keeps me smiling all day long.

Birds rest on my shoulders and they are my friends.

Never have I told anybody yet,

I have a crush on someone.

She lives in a small hut on the hillside.

She likes to wear a yellow dress,

Quietly sitting by the lakeside.

I can't speak a single word.
I can't walk a small step.
What I can do,
Watching her quietly on the sly.

On one night,
The sky was full of stars,
I had a dream:
I became a handsome young man,
Knocking on her door with a bunch of roses.
In the dime light of the dream,
So breathtaking she was.

(Translated by Niu Hai)

花雨纷飞的小径

这条花雨纷飞的小径

通往她的小屋

我看见含苞的紫薇花

慢慢绽放开她心底的秘密

一路飞舞的彩蝶

第二部分　眼前情愫
Part Two　A Love and Sincerity in My Mind

引我到她的家门口

她梨涡的浅笑
浓浓得甜了一片我的心田
她晶莹的目光
是悬在夜空中最明亮的星
那一条闪烁的银河很远　很长
这头是我
那头是她

A Path Covered with Rainy Flowers

It was a tiny narrow path,
To her small house with flowers of rain,
I saw that——
Jacarandas were blooming from her depth of heart.
A butterfly was dancing joyfully in this path.
I was attracted by its trace,
By her door, a kind of my hope stood.

Her smiles were like pear flowers,

Occupying my heart with great warmth.

Her charming eyes of glitter and translucence,

Like the brightest star in the sky of evening.

It was indeed a long sparkling Milky Way in the Galaxy.

Oh, I wanted to let her know——

That I was here at this side,

While she was on the other bank of the paradise.

爱情新纪元

我要主宰我的现在

我有我的年轻时代

不管一切勇敢去爱

让那热情全都回来

我在等待你的纯爱

梦幻未来星光成海

爱情咒语谁来解开

时空转换一切重来

第二部分　眼前情愫

你是我爱情的新纪元
是我人生的转折点
我感觉有你在身边
一切都会改变

爱情的新纪元
是我灿烂的生死恋
刻下永不悔的誓言
射出爱神的箭

（附注：这首诗原属于牛涛作词、作曲的歌曲《爱情新纪元》，由香港情歌王子李大卫演唱。歌曲一推出，便荣登QQ音乐巅峰人气榜。此处英译偏重于歌曲形式或节奏。）

A New Era, a Great Love

I have my own life today.
I want to be a master of great youth.
To love, for love, you are very brave,
Calling back that passion with immense.

I am waiting,

I am just waiting and waiting

Waiting for your great love, a pure love.

Future dream is at my hand,

And stars are shining into a honey land.

To call the love curse, whoever could be the next?

Time and space, let's travel across.

A new era comes.

You are my angel and goddess.

You are the turning point in my life.

Nobody else can take your place.

I can feel your pause and pace.

Everything will be perfect and nice.

A New Era, a Great Love

With your dazzling smile and brilliant love.

Forever love, forever young,

We sing a song of life and death along.

My heart is engraved with an oath.

Not a single of remorse.

Cupid gives us blessing.

Cupid's arrows send me golden sunshine.

第三部分　冥思天地间

Part Three　Mediation on Nature

午后涓涓的时光

午后涓涓的时光
在我眼底荡漾
那一朵花儿晒得低垂
好像一只慵懒的猫
绿油油的藤蔓
慢慢延伸
爬满我童年的岁月

午后悠悠的阳光
吻了一口山间的小湖
流年慢慢沉淀
荡涤在我的普洱茶杯中
透着艳阳的长廊
寂静悠长
通向温暖的午后梦乡

Cosy Time in the Afternoon

The trickling time in the afternoon,
Like ripples of my eyes.
Lower and lower, little by little,
The flower is falling to the ground,
Like a lazy sleepy cat.
Green vines can be slowly found,
Keeping my childhood company all the year round.

The afternoon sunshine seems to drag long,
A small lake was flowing between mountains.
Every mile and every year,
Time and distance quietly gone.
In my Pu'er tea cup, time is passing and floating.
A quiet corridor covered with golden sunshine,
I was enjoying a warm afternoon of my dreamland.

那一条山间小路

那一条山间小路
蜿蜒伸进白雾里
一个洁白的梦境
迷失了方向的我
俯首询问
一个在山麓歇息的老人家
绿叶间的彩蝶
生生世世
环绕她爱的那一朵野菊

那一条山间小路
跨过了
一条彩带般的小溪
我一脚踏空
差点跌进错落的树丛
没有人知道
有一个宋代诗人
此刻正立在
山顶雾里的那一座凉亭中

第三部分　冥思天地间
Part Three   Mediation on Nature

The Holzwege Among Mountain Tracks

There is a rough mountain track.
The holzwege winds its way to a white mist,
Falls into a white pure dreamland.
I lose my way because of the winding trail.
An old man is napping at the foot of the mountain.
I have to bow to him for my way-inquiring.
Where can I find colored butterflies in green foliage?
The wild chrysanthemum that she loves most,
Generation after generation is etched but never forgotten.

There is a rough mountain track,
Running across a colored ribbon brook.
I miss my steps when I go down the narrow road,
Dotted with green pines and cypresses.

No one knows that——
A Song Dynasty poet shaped like me,
Is now standing——
On a top mountain of pavilion among mist,
Finding her an acre of Heidegger's land.

随 想 曲

露水
是花朵哭泣的眼泪

夕阳
是天幕晕红的脸颊

彩虹
是给孩子们独家定制的滑梯

烟雨
是大地在盛夏撑起的一座蚊帐

第三部分 冥思天地间
Part Three Mediation on Nature

思念
是一条红线
这头是我
那边是你

A Piece of Capriccio

A drop of dew——
Is crying tears of the flower.

A sunset——
Is hung as red as the face of the sky.

A rainbow——
Is a slide fixed only for children.

The misty rain——
Is like a summer bed curtain.

A love medicine——
Is like a rose-pink line.
I am here on this side.

You are just on the other.

花　旦

弦声蓦然地响起
你登台一甩袖
甩出一地璀璨和痴迷
又一次入戏太深
分不清现实和剧情
沉醉在海潮般的掌声中

你是这戏院的当家花旦
大红大紫的时候
兴奋和狂热掩盖了悲伤
灯光一亮起
一开嗓
唱尽人间悲欢离合

等到这一出剧落幕了
等到人群都散尽了
卸妆后的你
只剩憔悴和疲惫

第三部分　冥思天地间
Part Three　Mediation on Nature

加上空虚惆怅的岁月

你又如何 你该怎么

面对这落幕后的

无尽人生

Hua Dan (A Female Role-Play in Chinese Drama)

With a sudden chord,

You embark and swing sleeves,

Swinging away brightness and obsession.

Because of a deep role into the drama,

You're unable to tell the reality from dream,

We're getting lost in the unremitting applauds.

You're Prima Donna in the theatre.

In the limelight, you're standing,

With your sadness covered by fanaticism.

Light's up and here you begin,

With the song of vicissitudes of life.

Till the curtain is put down,

Till the crowd is gone,

Till your mask is taken off,

You're left with tiredness and fatigue,

Just because of emptiness and melancholy.

What are you going to do?

And how do you face the endless days of your life——

When the show is over?

(Translated by Niu Hai)

飞 花

纷纷扬扬

半空中飞花

脱离了花枝

只这一刹的潇洒

落在你粉红色纸伞上

偷窥你比花绝美的脸庞

顷刻落入泥土中

任人践踏

即使碎成残缺花瓣

也要

美到生命的最后一刻

The Flying Flowers

The swirl of flowers here and there,

Dancing happily in the mid-air,

Running away from the branches,

For a moment of its real flair.

They left a pink tinge on your oiled-paper umbrella,

Keeping a nice peep at your beautiful face.

Even if flowers fell into the ground,

Even if they got trampled by others,

Even if they got broken into tiny petals,

They would, and they still——

Remain the immortal beautiful soul.

太 阳 雨

红日躲进了乌云中
掩面痛哭了一场

人间
下了一场太阳雨

我抬头望天涯
猜不透

A Sun Shower

A
Red sun
Is hiding in
The deep dark clouds.

He
Can not
Any longer
Hold his emotions in leash,
So that he comes to have a good cry.

In
This world,
There is a
Kind of sun shower with bright sunshine,
Even if I am looking up
At the further heavens.

I
Am not
Able to figure out
What is going to be on in the future
Under this very bright sun.

山水之间

清澈的湖面
驶过一艘天鹅船
泛起的波纹久久未平息
我站在湖边的亭子里
等春光 等微风 等烟雨

天空湛蓝得让人想流泪
云彩浮过山头
惹醉了一座青山

我想化作一条青鱼
往水更深处一直游
屏住一口气
游进一个迷幻幽暗的梦乡

第三部分　冥思天地间
Part Three　Mediation on Nature

在阳光下
闭上眼睛
听到时光流过的宁静
听见鲤鱼跃出湖面的水花声
甚至还听见未来
慢慢走近的声音

A Landscape in My Mind

In the clean still lake,
Came over a beautiful swan boat,
With waves and ripples curling from its sharp bow.
By the lakeside, I was standing in a pavilion,
To feel and touch misty rain, gentle breeze, and warm spring.

I was moved to tears because of the azure sky.
The clouds glowed like burnished gold,
Drifting silently over the hilltop up so high.
I was smitten by the landscapes of hills.

I wanted to change into a mackerel fish,

Keeping on swimming until I swam into the deeper lake.

I took a deeper breath,

Swimming again into a dreamland filled with illusion and darkness.

I closed my eyes under the sun,

Listening to the tranquility of the ticking-away times.

I listened again to the splashing sound,

Which was a carp fish jumping out of water.

I came to hear that——

Footsteps of bright future were approaching on and on.

And I began to realize that——

The macrocosm of the universe was——

Mirrored in the microcosm of the mind.

第三部分　冥思天地间
Part Three　Mediation on Nature

我站在风口

我站在风口

呼啸的北风把往事都带走

曾经一遍遍称呼的昵称

曾经爱神在清晨与黄昏的喃喃细语

请风把它们全带走吧

全部都带走

我站在风口

眼泪

滴在枯黄的落叶上

一地落叶

回旋在狂乱的风里

北风啊北风

你若是要去天涯海角

请你把我也带上——

把我带到——

那个没有悲伤眼泪的世界

I Am Standing in the Draught

I am standing in the draught.

The past events are blown away by the whistling North Wind.

And your lovely nickname that I used to call

第三部分　冥思天地间
Part Three　Mediation on Nature

you again and again,

A quiet sweet murmur from Cupid's blessing,

No matter it was made in the morning or in the evening.

I do beg you, the North Wind,

Please take them all away far behind,

Letting nothingness left in my mind.

I am standing in the draught.

My tears fall on the withered boughs.

Circling overhead in the wild wind,

The decaying leaves scatter over the ground.

Oh, the North Wind,

If you are going to the ends of the earth,

I beg, I do beg you,

I beg you to take me away far from the madding crowd,

Enjoying a utopia world of sorrows or tears without.

雨夜旅人

微凉的雨丝
斜斜地飘洒在风雨中
晚钟缓慢地
拨弄着时间
凄凉的夜色弥漫长街
一个穿黑色雨衣的行人
看不见容貌
低着头向前
一步一步走向长街的尽头
一场烟雨凄迷的幽梦

雨水
熄灭了满城的灯火
却浇不灭顽强的路灯
晚钟的时针
指向深夜
我撑一把孤零零的红雨伞
坐在钟塔下
默想 回味 忏悔 盼望

第三部分　冥思天地间
Part Three　Mediation on Nature

黑暗长街的深处
定然有一座晴朗的世外桃源
那是无数人的美丽梦境
交错成的幻梦城堡

狂风
吹翻我的雨伞
雨水
肆意冲刷我的面庞
此刻
我无能为力
雨水
交融着泪
我只是一个流落到此的诗人
我只是一个迷失雨夜的旅人

A Traveler on a Rainy Night

The gentle drizzle was chilly.

It was swirling in the air,

In the wind and rain,

The evening bell was slowly fiddling.

A dreary scenery overwhelmed me into the street end.

A pedestrian in a black raincoat,

With his invisible appearance,

His face was girded and forged ahead,

Step by step, little by little,

Towards the end of this long street.

For a dream of gloom and doom,

On this misty rainy night.

Heavy rain fell tightly at night.

The city lights went out, one after another.

And the dogged street lights could not be poured out.

The evening bell pointed its hour hand to a late night.

Holding a red umbrella with myself alone,

I was sitting under the Bell Tower in silence,

To contemplate, to repent, without anyone else,

Reliving the past, longing for the future.

At the dark street corner,

第三部分　冥思天地间
Part Three　Mediation on Nature

There must be a bright Shangri-La,

Which built up endless beautiful dreamland.

And a fantasy castle was crisscrossed.

A violent wind blew my umbrella over to the ground.

The rain swept away my face in a big mess.

Right at this moment,

I was too weak to do anything else.

Rain soaked into my tears.

I was only a poet,

Wandering around to the end of the street.

I was actually a lost traveler on this rainy night.

煮茶雨夜

静心

煮一壶浓浓的普洱

水雾

升腾起一股禅意

沉淀着

月光般的宁静

帘外
细雨敲打着芭蕉
往事
一如蜿蜒的石板路
越走越深
越走越迷离

我饮一口香茶
陶醉了满心的愁绪
茶香
透过雨帘
净化了这一方世界

合上读了一晚的书卷
饮尽泡了一晚的香茶
我慢慢坠入梦境
抬头看见
梦里的故乡

第三部分　冥思天地间
Part Three　Mediation on Nature

Tea-Making on a Rainy Night

I brewed a pot of strong Pu'er tea.
A magic sense of Zen rose with mist,
Adding gradually to the moonlight tranquility.

The gentle drizzle outside the curtain,
The banana leaves were rhythmically rattling.
The past events were like the zigzag lanes with stone slabs.
The further to go, the deeper to find,
And the deeper to see, the more blurred and muddled it would be.

I took a sip of the fragrant tea,
Dispelling all my gloom and melancholy.
A tea aroma released from the rain curtain,
Purifying this world with refresh peace.

I closed a book that I read all night around.

I tasted fragrant tea that was brewed on and on.
I was leisurely caught in a sweet dream,
Catching sight of my beautiful hometown.

品　茶

浓茶半杯
化不开半生
苦涩的记忆
我闭上眼
喝一口
想你的味道
暖风
把揉碎的阳光
洒在我身上
一点一点 温暖地
往心里渗

记忆里的那张凳子
似乎曾经有一个人
如今

第三部分　冥思天地间
Part Three　Mediation on Nature　　173

人也消失了

风也无力了

水也安静了

孤单的柳絮

一点一点

凄凉地

往心里飘

Tea-Tasting

Half a cup of very strong tea,

Cannot simply brew bitter memory,

Of the half lifetime of me.

I close my eyes,

Having a drop of tea soup in my mouth,

Tasting a flavor of my thoughts about you.

Warm winds have modulated the sun into golden bright.

I can feel the sunlight spreading in my heart.

There is a stool in my memory,

Someone seemed to bring me happiness and merry.

But nowadays,

I could not find her among the crowds.

Even the wind has no power to resist.

Water has no vigour for a free flow.

Only the willow catkins are fluttering alone,

Little by little,

Roaming in its bitterness

Into my desolated heart.

白马与孤客

白马放逐天际

第三部分　冥思天地间

Part Three　Mediation on Nature

孤客浪迹天涯

白马不懂孤客的悲寂

孤客不晓白马的疲累

但若是

长路上相逢

它与他也定会

依偎在一起

孤客老了

迎风叹出悠长的叹息

白马老了

眼里泛着浊蒙的泪水

A White Horse and a Lonely Traveler

A white horse is running under the sky.

A lonely traveler is roaming in the world.

The white horse doesn't understand the sorrow of the lonely traveler,

The lonely traveler doesn't understand the hardship of the white horse.

But if they meet each other on the long way,

They will possibly be snuggling together.

The lonely traveler gets old, taking a deep sigh towards the wind.

The white horse gets old, with turbid tears in his eyes.

(Translated by Niu Hai)

苦 海

汹涌的海浪

冲毁我内心的堤岸

我用海沙为你盖的那座城堡

也在一瞬间粉身碎骨

我任自己在汪洋中漂流

路过了忧郁的蓝鲸

路过了沉默的珊瑚礁

但愿能遇见你的航船

救起奄奄一息的我

Part Three Mediation on Nature

An Abyss of Misery

A rogue wave,

Swamped the bank of my mind.

I built you a castle with the sand on the seashore.

But it was smashed to pieces as quickly as a flash.

I found myself to be driven by the boundless current in the sea,

Passing by the melancholy blue whale,

Passing through the silent coral reef.

If only I could have been on your life ship,

If only you could rescue me at my last gasp.

Because without your true love,

My life would be just a still ship without a rudder, an empty body without a soul!

海　恋

五彩气泡在升腾
蓝色水浪
窒息了梦境
悲伤在下沉
心碎声被掩盖

可我还在奋力向你游
故事别在此刻终结
我还有好多话没说
就算是寒冰冻结天地
就算我困在冰点三天三夜

想你流下的
那一滴滚烫的热泪
也足以顷刻融化冰山

你本是
翩翩美人鱼也罢
你本是

第三部分 冥思天地间
Part Three Mediation on Nature

冰雪王国的公主也好

还没遇见你
怎么能就这样
沉到海底长眠

A Love Song of the Sea

Colorful bubbles keep on rising,
Like a silent lubricant.
Blue waves keep rising,
And my dreams are also capsizing.

Down with a big grief,
Up with a broken heart of my soul,
I am in my persistence still
Swimming so hard that——
I am trying to be close to you.

The story might not end with our goal,
Because many words have been left to go.
The heavy ice is frozen, though——

I would prefer to be trapped in the frozen ices, day and night.

Hot tears in your eye are running down,

Too much enough to melt the icebergs at once.

I just can't help wondering——

If you are a mermaid of the sea,

Or you are the princess of the Ice Kingdom.

Since I haven't met you before,

How could you have your heart——

To sink for a sleepless dream in the sea-bottom?

初 春

冲破了迷雾

我的列车

在正午

抵达了春天的深处

柳絮

把故事里的泪光与笑语

第三部分　冥思天地间
Part Three　Mediation on Nature

洋洋洒洒地飘满大地

我躺在

绿水上的小船

直面无穷的苍穹

幻化作了一场云烟

鸟雀

飞上碧空

一曲天籁

惊醒人世

春天来了

The Dancing Steps of Spring Season

Through the mist of winter,

A blurred carriage——

Arrived at midday,

In the inner heart of spring.

Tears are shed.

Laughter and smiles burst out,

Floating like catkins in my mind.

Dancing in the air,

Napping on the ground,
I am lying on the boat with aqua.
Looking out to the infinite castle in the sky,
Until the old seasons have changed,
And changed into a vapor.

Swallows are flying over the blue clouds.
A sonata from the nature,
Playing a great Strauss melody for the spring!

七月天默想

繁华夏花
一路绚烂地绽开
斑斓
渲染了我暗淡的眼眸
记忆里
总有一个你
远远站着 嫣然不语

斑驳的香樟树影
摇晃着阳光

第三部分　冥思天地间
Part Three   Mediation on Nature

我坐在浓荫下
静默听蝉鸣
记忆里
总有一个你
穿着白裙
从这条林荫道经过

热烈的艳阳
散落成水面的碎金
快要煮沸了
一整湖的愁绪
记忆里
总有一个你
穿插在我的脑海里
一次次的春夏秋冬

Meditation on Days in July

Splendid summer flowers,

Keep on blooming but never rest.

Colors and radiance glisten upon my blurry eyes.

In the process of my wandering memory,

You are always my sweet story,

Part Three Mediation on Nature

Pulling away from me with a distant,

Sending me your dazzling smiles,

Which is hard to misunderstand.

The dappled shade of camphor tree,

The sun was overshadowed to see

Sitting in the shade, I am listening to the chirping of cicadas,

I'm just keeping silent at ease.

In the process of my wandering memory,

You always belong to my sweet story.

I see you enjoy wearing a pure white dress,

Along that boulevard, gracefully to pass.

The bright sun is hanging over the blue sky,

Scattering golden fragments over boundless surface of lakes.

The lake is almost boiled over by melancholy thoughts.

In the process of my wandering memory,

You are always my sweet story.

Your images would be threaded into numbers of lines.

I'd like very much to share with you.
The peaceful alternation of four seasons.

深秋明月夜

深秋的凉风
呼啸了整夜
黄叶还沾着
盛夏艳阳的余温
短暂如烟花
便凋落成灾

明月失眠了
晚星难入睡了
伴着我
呆坐在小花园
无言共对
树影婆娑
冷风掠过
掩住我小径深处的落泪声

呆坐到夜已阑珊

第三部分　冥思天地间
Part Three　Mediation on Nature

红着眼

望着月亮的脸

那么美 那么亮

A Moon-Night in Late Autumn

There comes a late-autumn cool breeze,
Whistling over and over all night.
The yellow leaves are stained with the lingering bright of the sun,
In a state of decay, they are falling down,
Like fireworks to be so far gone.

The bright moon suffers from insomnia.
The melancholy stars begin to blink and peep here and there,
Becoming my pal in a small garden.
I'm sitting there with a lonely heart.
Not a single word can I have in common.
The shadows of trees are dancing.
A current of cool air is blowing,
Drowning the sound of my sob at a path end.

I am sitting there, idling away with my time,
Till night comes to an end.
I can feel myself blush,
Looking at the face of the moon.
She is blessing us a so beautiful shine!

入冬以后

我系上了
你为我织的白围巾
我抚摸着
毛线茸茸的感觉
就好像
触摸到你温暖的指尖

窗台上的布娃娃
一声声问我你去了哪里
你叫我如何回答才是好

飘雪的深冬
冰封了多少个梦境

第三部分 冥思天地间
Part Three Mediation on Nature

结晶了多少滴眼泪

我怕我会熬不过

这个漫长深夜

又一次白色的

孤独世界

Late Winter

The white scarf you knitted for me last year,

I tied it warmly round my neck this year.

I gently stroke the wool with a feeling of soft and sweet,

As if I am touching your warm finger tips.

Dolls on the windowsill,

Asking me with a long sigh.

"Hey, guy, where have you been?"

I really do not know,

How to respond this to you.

The heavy snow is falling down,

No one knows how many frozen dreams can

be kept on.

No one knows how many snow-iced crystals of tears are made from.

And I'm afraid I will not get through this cold,

Just in this white snow world.

The long long chilly cold night——

Will be another lonely and solitary life for me to lead.

雪　夜

雪花
在昏黄的路灯中飘坠
迅速掩盖了
一个下班工人的自行车印
古老的蒸汽机车
慢慢消失在夜雾中

在望不到尽头的湖面中
我打捞起一段失落的故事
几束无力的灯光

第三部分 冥思天地间
Part Three Mediation on Nature

锻造出雪的腰身

一行沉默的山羊
正在往西边走
走向
一段陌生的时光

A Snowy Night

Under the dim light of the street lamp,
The snowflake, fell to the ground all over,
Leaving no traces of bicycle by an off-duty worker.
An old steam locomotive of the long long time——
Came to vanish with a mist of the night.
I picked up an old story of my youth lost
From the endless surface of a lake.
The waist line of snow was built then——
By some very weak light.

A group of silent sheep were going to the

west,

Left me with their unusual time far and fast.

雪　域

半空中
飘下了雪花
宁静的十二月
在一片纯白中晶莹闪烁

雪地上
存留着
昨夜孩子们玩耍的脚印
一个憨厚的雪人
在寒风中伫立
守护这纯洁的童年

我翻开古老的诗集
诗中正描写
某个十二月的清晨
从雪地上走过
雪一样的清纯女子

第三部分　冥思天地间
Part Three   Mediation on Nature

The Snowy Land

Snowflakes are dancing freely in the air.

A tranquil December is coming right here,

Twinkle, twinkle, all white pure,

Glittering with little stars.

In the snowy land,
Footprints are deeply remained,
Because kids were playing a snowball fight last night.
A simple honest snow man is——
Standing against the cold wind,
Who protects this pure childhood zealously.

I opened an old collection of poems.
In the poems,
A poet is lost in meditation on the peaceful December morning:
A girl is walking through the snowy land,
Looking up to be as pure as the White Snow Prince,
Keeping her red dress with a gentle breeze.

林 荫 道

我喜欢这里的林荫道

第三部分　冥思天地间
Part Three Mediation on Nature

一排排不知名的树
红的叶 黄的叶
<u>丝丝</u>缕缕地
遮挡着澄蓝的天空

我爱着这里的林荫道
你走在前面 我走在后面
深一脚 浅一脚
就像童年那条放学的路

我记住了
这里的林荫道
我等你
回眸的那一刻
遇见你纯净的目光
冷的风 骤的雨
洗不尽
这儿绚烂如初的华彩

A Boulevard Lined with Trees

I am enjoying a boulevard near my place.

Rows of nameless trees are well lined with.

The leaves are a patch work of the red and yellow.

I am quietly enjoying these faint trace strands of the peace.

The larks are soaring highly in the blue sky with a hope.

I am enjoying a boulevard near my place.

You are going ahead, and I am following your pace,

Staggering in a zigzag across the road.

It seems to recapture all the sweet memories from my childhood.

A boulevard is almost buried in my mind,

A glance of your back fascinates me with a sweet smile,

And your eyes are so pure and clean,

That even if the cold wind and the heavy rain——

Can not wear off brilliant colors on the roadside.

第三部分　冥思天地间
Part Three　Mediation on Nature

夜

夜深了
人踏着星光
夜色迷蒙中
遗落了泪光

夜静了
人迎着晚风
涛声澎湃中
走丢了梦境

A Night Wears On

A night——
Is getting darker and darker.
A man——
Is rambling on under the starlight.
The night is dreary and hazy.
He feels a little bit lost in my eyes.

A night——

Is deadly quiet.

A man——

Is ruffled against the evening breeze.

When he is listening to the sound of waves,

He should have forgotten all of his beautiful dreams.

小园雨夜

散了
午夜的香梦
窗外
一场细雨如烟
把我的梦惊断

凝望无边的夜空
冷静静的水面
一片淡月
被细雨打碎

夜雨落着

第三部分　冥思天地间
Part Three Mediation on Nature

路上
一缕轻烟
如梦地
在雨中蔓延
缠住了谁人的醉意

雨中
带一曲琴声
是谁还未眠
弄一曲清音细雨声

雨点
打在荷塘
荡一片雨花
在青烟中袅袅起舞

雨停
荷花上
点着几滴珠露
人在倦意中
飘向梦境
梦里
迁出一个恬淡的心境

A Rainy Night at a Small Garden

Sweet dreams at midnight have finally gone.

A drizzle outside the window was falling down,

Shocking me up with my broken heart upon.

I gazed out over the limitless expanse of sky, feeling cold with fear.

A dim moon was lying on the still water.

The gentle breeze dimpled water into blue ripples.

Tonight the rain was falling down.

A thin wisp of smoke straggled upon to the ground.

In my dream alike,

The unquenchable yearning was spreading on this endless night.

A light melody was played around in the rain.

第三部分 冥思天地间
Part Three Mediation on Nature

Whoever was sleepless at this moment,
Plucking to play with a clear sound of violin.

The little raindrops were beating against the lotus pond,
Stirring up ripples to the water surface around,
Dancing gracefully in the misty breeze.

The rain left off near and far,
The drops of dew were on the lotus flower.
Sleepy and sluggish, I was on my tour to a dreamland,
Enjoying a tranquility of life right at hand.

一 半

天空上
一半是黑云
一半是白云

湖水上
一半是碧波

一半是静水

你脸上
一半是晕红
一半是黯淡

我心里
一半是你
另一半还是你

One Half

In the sky,
One half is black clouds,
The other is white clouds.

Over the sparkling lake,
One half is green-waves,
The other is blue water in clean.

On your face,
Glow and gloom has its equal shares.

第三部分　冥思天地间
Part Three　Mediation on Nature

In my heart,

One half is you,

The other half is the absolute only you.

孤　寂

我的世界

安静得可怕

孤寂的小屋

孤寂的书桌

写满寂寞诗行的诗

静静地摊开着

我是

一只沉默不语的羔羊

站在黑夜的草原

眺望远方的灯火辉煌

无奈又无助

我被困黑暗而无法逃脱

短短一生

几次缘来缘又尽

等到一天
我要永远离开
你来看看我心房
空空荡荡的小屋
却还挂着一张
你曾经
笑得最甜的旧照

The Solitude of My Life

What a world of my life!
It is dreadfully peaceful,
With a small desk at a small room.
Lonely lines make up with my poems.
They are lying quietly on the small desk.

I am wordlessly as silent as a lamb,
Standing on the grass lands in the dark,
Looking up so far at brilliant lights.
But I have no choice to make,
And I have to be trapped in the darkness with no way to escape.

I hate to look back to my short life time,

Because Fate is a thing that easy comes, easy goes.

Till one day I am going to leave away with you.

You can come to see what dwells in my mind.

An empty hut with nothing fun,

Only a picture of yours once to be hung on,

Your sweet smiles in the old photo is as bright as the sun.

古镇随笔

蜿蜒在古镇的小径
通往一个诗人的旧宅
我眼前淡雾迷离
淋了一身栀子花雨

万家灯笼
点亮了迟暮时光
我静默看着
街角的老人家

无声眺望着远山
又翻起许多
陈旧的 泛黄的往事

小湖上的涟漪
荡漾开了淡月的波光
我走到小路的尽头
能否
在一位诗人的梦境里
借住一宿

Capriccio of a Town

The path circles around miles of the tranquil town,

Towards a poet's old house.

The path is stretched down.

My eyes were blurred with a milky mist.

I was caught in the rain of blossoms all garden around.

Thousands of thousands lanterns lit up the

Part Three Mediation on Nature

twilight,

I looked at the street corner without words.

Looking out to the hills so far,

To dredge up their yellowish past events.

The ripples on the lake——

Glistened into dim moonlight under the dark.

I walked to the end of the path,

Asking myself with a sigh:

If, or perhaps if——

I could put up for just one night,

I might have made my dream in a poet's dreamland.

酒 吧 街

喧闹的酒吧街

撒一抹霓虹

在长岛冰茶里

流浪歌手

弹着老旧的木吉他

在拐角唱了一晚

只有
那顶牛仔帽里
放了几枚零散的硬币

整座城市
已经陷入沉睡
而狂热的梦
像一朵五彩的毒花
闪烁着
异样吸引人的亮光
在酒杯里绽放婀娜

我已渐渐有了醉意
耳边
是舒缓的英式摇滚
愁绪
在酒杯里溺亡
有关于过去的岁月
绝口不提
我是狂欢中
黑暗的一角
最孤独的过客

Part Three Mediation on Nature

A Bar Street

The raucous laughter from the bar street,
The neon lights flashed in turns at night.
In an Iced Tea Room of the Long Island,
A traveling singer was playing an old wooden guitar,
Singing at the street corner all night long.
But nothing was left in the air,
Only some coins in the cowboy's hat.

Even if the whole city,
Had fell into a fast sleep.
I was still crazy about my fancy dreams,
Blossomed like a poison of beautifully colored flowers,
Glittering with amazing light,
Swaying gracefully in the glass of wine.

I was feeling slightly tipsy with beer.
An English Rock'n'Roll seemed to have soft

power,

Coming near little by little to my ear.

Sadness was melted away in the glass of wine.

I kept the past events in my mind,

Not a single word was to be mentioned.

Because I was just——

A passer-by in this Dionysian ecstasy,

Standing at the street corner with my lonely heart.

温 泉

一池温泉

煮熟了

一颗橘红的夕阳

沸腾的泉眼

翻滚着

几瓣玫瑰花瓣

木屋檐下

红红的灯笼

第三部分 冥思天地间
Part Three Mediation on Nature

最暖的泉水

在花园小径最深处

加了牛奶的泉水

泛腾着

微微的水雾

如笑容一般甜

日落之后

空无一人的园林

只剩下

泉眼还在翻腾

园中的花蝴蝶

扑翅飞入了

我梦里的花园

A Pool of Spring Water

An reddish orange sunset,

Was boiled by a pool of spring water.

A few rose petals were bubbled in the springs.

Under the eaves,

The Spring water mixed with red lanterns,

Hung in the deepest path of the garden.

The milked spring water looked like a faint mist.

Its smiling face appeared to be a honey sweet.

After a sunset,

In an empty garden, everyone had left.

Only the mouth of a spring was billowing yet.

The colorful butterflies were dancing in the garden,

Flapping into my dreamland of gorgeous garden.

纸 船

浓绿的花园那边

是一条绿色的溪流

没有锦鲤 没有波澜

只承载着我的

一只单薄的纸船

第三部分 冥思天地间
Part Three Mediation on Nature

纸船

划出两道涟漪

逆着风

去追天边的云彩

展开

我梦的版图

碾着

一道霞光的轨迹

挣脱悲伤的水潮

你看

那小纸船

载着希望 载着春光

也一样有巨轮的光芒

A Paper Boat

Over the dark green garden,
There was a brook with all green,
No pretty koi fish, no great waves,
Carrying my little paper boat only.

Two ripples were quivering across the brook.

It was just against the wind,

To chase the clouds in the sky,

To expand my dreamland behind.

A paper boat was mirrored by the glory of God at dawn,

Which made the tide of sadness so clean.

Oh, can't you find this paper boat——

Carrying my youth with great hope,

Like a big ship ploughed with golden gleam,

Across the ocean, across the ocean,

Keep going forward, without any stopping!

月 亮 船

弯月

是一艘晚点的小船

悠悠摇晃

在天上的柔波里

云霞涌上来

化作浪 浪打着浪

载着我去找你

第三部分　冥思天地间
Part Three   Mediation on Nature   215

我乘着月亮船

驶过一个又一个国度

可是

你如今

流浪去了哪一方

还是

没有看见你的身影

还是

没有听到你的声音

等到破晓时分

船也破碎了

云海也消弭了

把我搁浅在天穹上

无路可退

The Moon Boat

A crescent moon,

Looks like a delayed boat.

In the gentle waves of the blue sky,

A boat is rocked to poke on between.

The rosy clouds stand out against the waves.
Waves after waves lapping against the boat,
Waiting for me with great patience,
Picking me up to your admiring paradise.

I'm on my journey by the moon boat,
Traveling over from one country to another.
But nowadays,
Where have you been to lead a vagrant life?

I am listening over and over,
But I have nowhere to see your figure.
I try hard to listen,
But not a single sound can be heard.
Until the sunny day is coming,
Until the boat has broken,
Until the sea of clouds has gone,
In the vault of heaven,
I have to find myself running around,
No way to retreat but to keep on and on.

第三部分　冥思天地间
Part Three　Mediation on Nature

今夜 我在吉隆坡

今夜 我在吉隆坡
双峰塔斑斓泻影在我窗上
等到这杯冰咖啡饮尽
等到整条街的车马歇了喧闹
入夜多寂寥

今夜 我在吉隆坡
繁华街灯下
满眼是异乡的面孔
哪怕几句熟悉的乡音
也存在我心坎里
仿佛中听见有人用华语说：
"我爱你！"

今夜 我在吉隆坡
夜半难眠 我在窗口望繁星
隔着飘纱之外
双峰塔也睡熟了
也许

那个明月升起的方向
就是我故乡

I'm in Kuala Lumpur Tonight

I'm in Kuala Lumpur tonight,
The shadows of the Petronas Twin Towers are gorgeous,
Casting a soft radiance over my window.
Hardly have I finished this iced coffee,
When the street din gradually dies down.
The solitude and silence fills me all around.

第三部分 冥思天地间
Part Three   Mediation on Nature

I'm in Kuala Lumpur tonight,

Under the street lamps of this busiest street,

Different colors of skins and faces shock me at once.

Even if I understand a few words of familiar accent,

I am proud to imprint them in my mind.

I seem to hear someone speak in Chinese,

Blurting a sound of "I love you" in a sentence.

I'm in Kuala Lumpur tonight,

In the middle of the night,

I am staring up at the starry sky by the window,

Through the window screening outside.

The Petronas Twin Towers falls into fast sleep.

Perhaps, or it must be——

A direction from where the bright moon rises,

Carrying a homesick message from my lips.

年末遐想

听晚风
诉说一座城的故事
玉兰花雨
飘飘洒洒
灿烂了小路的尽头
透过窗
接一捧月光
淘洗我蒙尘的回忆

一杯浓酒
饮醉了一串往事
是飞花还是烟雨
笼罩我孤单的梦魂

一整夜
在梦里流离失所
在门口来回地踱步
杂乱的思绪
纠缠在一起

第三部分 冥思天地间
Part Three　Mediation on Nature

锁住我的胸口

把悲伤的记忆

系在气球上

升上无极的夜空

One More Year Has Gone

Listen, Oh, listen——

The evening breeze is telling me a story of a city,

Down the drifting rain of Mongolia flowers,

Glittering here and there,

Stretching out to the end of a long path.

A handful moonlight through my window,

Ridding off dusty memories of my hope.

A cup of liquor,

Made me drunk with a string of old days.

I just doubt about:

Are they a lonely heart with flying flowers or with rains of mist?

My lonely heart is at a big loss,

Something on my mind rose up, as vivid as a movie all over the night,

Like an aimless wanderer in the dark.

And confused ideas often get mixed together,

Knocking me out like cold chains.

I get to find that——

Those bitter memories are tied to a balloon,

Ascending to the Infinite of the Sky.

Listen, Oh, listen again:

For You and Me, God is quietly sobbing!

十 年

十年之前

久远的故事

是镜框里泛黄的笑容

是书架上陈旧的日记

有些人经过

有些人离开

还有些人

常驻在心间

第三部分 冥思天地间
Part Three Mediation on Nature

十年的笑声 哭声

在我耳边盘旋

光阴的列车

驶过了

再也不回头

十年之后

我又

会在哪里呢

Ten Years Later

This is an old story ten years ago:

My yellowish smile in the photo,

A diary on the shelf turned out to be old.

Someone chose to pass by,

Someone chose to go away,

Still others chose to be buried forever in my heart.

Ten years with laughter and tears,

Hovering over into my ears.

There comes the Time Train,

Once it passes by, never does it come again.

Ten years later,

Where shall I be?

I just can't help wondering.

晚　祷

十字架

闪烁着温暖与慈悲

我翻阅另一章《圣经》

夜幕下的晚祷啊

淹没在浓雾中

我问主

如今祂身处天涯哪一方

祂如今快乐或苦困

三年了啊　我的命运

时刻与祂紧紧捆绑着

在圣光中转身

依稀还见祂穿一身白裙

笑得那般好温暖

第三部分　冥思天地间
Part Three　Mediation on Nature

我抓不住 抓不住
祂转眼湮没在骤起的烟雨中

我问主
你牵起万千条纯洁姻缘
我问主啊
你为何偏偏让她远走天涯
今夜我跪在教堂 泪流满面

我求主啊 我求主
让我再一次见见祂
只求再见祂一面

Night Prayer

The Cross was shining with warmth and mercy,

I read over the next chapter of the *Bible*.

The evening prayers in the darkness were drowned in the thick fog.

I asked the Lord:

Where are you now?

Do you ever have a happy life?

It has been three years for my fate,
It has been tied to Lord every now and then.
Turning back in the holy light,
I saw Lord dimly in a white dress still.
His smile is sweet and warm,
But I can't catch Him though.
He was drowned in the sudden rain.

I asked my Lord,
Piles and piles of marriages from you.
I asked my Lord,
Why did you just let her go?
I knelt in the church tonight,
With tears covered my face.

I pray, I pray, I pray to my Lord!
Please let me see her once more,
Please let me see her once more.

(Translated by Niu Hai)

第三部分　冥思天地间
Part Three　Mediation on Nature

夜 城 堡

明月光

洒成满地霜

诗集里

一抹我的泪光

灵魂左岸

有绽放的花火

照亮命运彼岸

未知的苦与乐

那是闪电和春雷

劈开你尘封的心门

音乐声 轰鸣般响起

神圣的命运 骤然开场

我拉着你

踩着一路的荆棘

逃离这喧闹的城堡

在那目光可及的远方

是我们恋爱的天堂

Night Castle

The bright moonlight,

Spreading over like frost on the floor.

In the poetry, my glistening tear drops,

In the left bank of my soul,

Blooming a kind of fireworks,

Lightening the opposite shore of destiny,

Where is full of unknown joys and sorrows.

It was lightening,

It was spring thunder,

That rived your dusty heart.

Sound of music, played as high as a roar,

Divine heritage started all of a sudden.

I was holding your hand in my arms,

With thorns all the way forward,

Far from this noisy castle,

To the place as far as the eye could reach,

Where is Our paradise of our great love!

(Translated by Niu Hai)

第三部分　冥思天地间
Part Three　Mediation on Nature

东瀛故事

日本姑娘啊

我道一句"沙哟娜拉"

此生再见

或许只在一个

樱花纷飞如雨的梦乡

到时

你记得

穿一身粉紫色的和服

到时

我肯定学会用日语说

"我想你了"

玄米茶的雾气

升腾起清澈的禅意

你身穿端庄的和服

低垂着秀气的眉眼

我猜不透

你的身世 你的心事

第三部分　冥思天地间
Part Three　Mediation on Nature

长满青苔的石板路

留下谁人木屐的脚印

这一条小路

樱花雨扬扬纷飞

通向一个木造的小屋

讲述一串古老又恬淡的

东瀛故事

My Stories in Japan

To my Japanese girl,

I am going to say さようなら.

To see you again for this life,

Maybe only,

In a dream where, sakura petals are flying like rain.

When that time comes,

Please remember that——

To wear a suit of pink and purple kimono.

When that time comes,

I will definitely learn to say one sentence in Japanese:"あいたい".

The fog of Genmaicha,

Is rising clear Buddhist mood.

You are in an elegant kimono,

With beautiful eyes and eyebrows down.

I am unable to make out,

Your story, or what is on your mind.

Part Three　Mediation on Nature

On the mossy slate road,

Whose footprints of clogs are left?

The sakura rain is falling down all over the path,

Stretching out to a wooden hut at ease.

A string of ancient and halcyon Japanese stories.

(Translated by Niu Hai)

译后记

两年前的一个冬天,广州特别的湿冷,于是,我便选择去云南腾冲过冬。这次出远门,特意带上了青年诗人牛涛在香港出版的一本小诗集。在腾冲,我每天的生活基本上就是晒晒太阳,喝喝普洱,读读小诗,什么也不想,什么也不做,日子虽然略显单调沉闷了些,倒过得很悠闲、很惬意。不经意间,一个冬天下来,越读牛涛的小诗,我就越觉得他的诗写得挺真、挺美、挺亲切。恰好,时值有美国朋友聊起了在海外孔子学院(学堂)推广中国诗歌和中国文化一事,于是,我便萌生出要英译青年诗人牛涛现代诗歌的想法。

记得当时,我正好还捎带了一本哈罗德·布鲁姆(Harold Bloom,1930～2019)写的《读诗的艺术》(*The Art of Reading Poetry*,2005)。布鲁姆这个睿智的美国小老头在这本书中,就诗歌的本质、诗歌的伟大、诗歌的力量等诸多问题做了非常精彩、有趣的论述和分析。布鲁姆认为,诗歌本质上是比喻性的语言,由于它集中凝练,故其形式兼具表现力和启示性。而诗歌之所以伟大,则在于其依靠比喻性语言的神采和认知的力量。诗歌的力量则在于:它把思想和记忆十分紧密地融合在一起,以至于我们无法把这两种过程分割开来。因为诗性的记忆使"相认"(Recognition)成为一种可能,其实也就是一种发现(Anagnorisis)。布鲁姆似乎强调过,在一首具有真正力量的诗歌写作过程中,作者都必须要回顾一首更早的诗,无论这首诗是出自诗人本人之笔,还是出自别人之笔。这种相认的过程,使得诗性的思考被诗与诗之间的影响带到了具体的语境之中。布鲁姆更是引用了英国玄学派诗人约翰·邓恩(John Donne, 1572~1631)的一首诗《圣露西节的夜祷》(*A Nocturnal upon St. Lucy's Day*)来说明:一种爱何以能让诗人复活在毁灭中。

Study me then, you who shall lovers be.

At the next world, that is, at the next spring.

For I am every dead thing,

In whom love wrought new alchemy.

For his art did express,

A quintessence even from nothingness,

From dull privations, and lean emptiness.

He ruin'd me, and I am re-begot

Of absence, darkness, death; things which are not.

应该说,正是布鲁姆睿智的思想和精辟的诗歌分析,坚定了我英译牛涛现代诗的决心。不仅如此,在我长达二十多年的英美文学教学生涯中,我尤其钟爱英国湖畔派诗人(Lake Poets)和美国诗人罗伯特·弗洛斯特(Robert Frost,1874～1963)。湖畔派诗人对大自然的那种热爱和激情,令人感怀。他们认为所有的好诗都是强烈情感的自然流露(The Spontaneous Overflow of Powerful Emotion)。诗人是人性最坚强的保护者、支持者和维护者。诗人用语言去描写日常生活,去抒发人间真情和友谊。弗洛斯特谈诗的一句名言"始于愉悦,终于智慧"(begins with pleasure and ends in wisdom)及名诗《未选择的路》(*The Road Not*

Taken),无论何时何地,都能让我常读常新,传诵难忘。英国浪漫派诗人威廉·华兹华斯(William Wordsworth,1770~1850)强调指出,写诗之人至少应该具备五种能力:第一是观察和描绘的能力;第二是感受力;第三是沉思;第四是想象力,也就是改变、创造和联想的能力;第五是对人和事的判断力。

无独有偶,中国古人也有很多谈论诗歌创作的心得名句,如"在心为志,发言为诗"。毋庸置疑,"诗言志"几乎成了千百年来中国历代诗人自觉或不自觉的一种诗歌创作主张。青年诗人牛涛的现代诗歌创作,在某种程度上充分实践了古人的这一诗歌创作主张,契合我喜欢的英美诗人之诗风,带给读者满满的正能量和美美的体验。

当被问到为什么要用诗歌的形式去表达自己的感情时,一向腼腆低调的牛涛一下子就变得满怀深情,言语中难以抑制他的真诚和激情。每逢这种场合,他总是情难自禁地告诉别人说:"我10岁就开始写诗了,觉得诗可以记录我的情绪感受。我看很多诗,徐志摩的、戴望舒的。当同学们还不知道什么是现代诗的时候,我就开始读诗了。"在牛涛眼里,生活中有很多令他感动的事,他生怕自己会忘记这些事,所以,他就选择用诗来记录生活点滴,以给后人以思考和启发。牛涛还经常慷慨地透露自己的写诗小秘诀:"我写诗,通常会一段段地去铺垫,情绪会随之逐渐浓烈。诗的最后,往往会将感情推向高潮。当我每次写到有关亲人和朋友的诗时,会写到我自己都忍不住要哭出来为止。"

正是本着这份真诚的写诗主张,牛涛的现代诗总能够给读者美好的希望和甜蜜的回忆。读者读他的诗歌,如同欣赏爱情电影,总会在不经意间体会到各种欣喜感、惊奇感和甜蜜感。当然,这些感觉并不是一成不变、波澜不惊的。开始,它是一种愉悦的情愫,偏向于激情和冲动。而当他写下第一行以后,他的诗情画意便有了流向;之后便是文思泉涌地一行接着一行;最后,在对人生思考以及那种天人合一的意境中收尾。牛涛的诗歌创作,是那种自然而然、水到渠成的最本真的情感表达,鲜有那种丧失了诗味的炫技和雕琢。如果诗人不含着泪写,读者就不会含着泪读。写诗之人既然没有内心惊喜,读诗之人也绝不会打心眼里觉得有趣。这就是我精心选择牛涛现代诗歌来英译的初衷和心愿。我希望能够借助于英语翻译这种媒介,把牛涛用他手中之笔记录下来的那些感人瞬间传播给更多的海外读者,尤其是那些对当代中国感兴趣的外国友好人士。

诚然诗歌创作需要真情实感,诗歌英译何尝不是如此呢?事实上,汉语诗歌的英译,其难度和挑战自不待言。中外学界的各路名家历来都有"诗不可译"之类的无休止争论。有人甚至惊呼"Translation is a betrayal",觉得译诗是一件出力不讨好的事情。上海青年女诗人包慧怡博士以其对中世纪"珍珠诗人"手稿的研究和翻译心得提出了独特看法。她认为,翻译中近乎体力劳作的部分,那份类似于打坐的心无旁骛,让她免于巨大的挫败感所带来的频繁崩溃。在包慧怡看来,翻译自己喜爱诗人的作品,是对其自身语言感受性的持续侵略、扩充与更新。好诗近巫,不仅演绎语言的无穷可能性,也向存在的森林推开一扇星光之门。就此而言,汉语诗歌的英译也并不像某些翻译理论家说得那么"玄乎"。就大多数情况而言,汉诗英译不应该对原诗进行字斟句酌的过度推敲,而应该力求做到与原作者"心有灵犀一点通",在充分领会原作者写诗情感和创作意图的基础上,完全理解了诗歌源语之后,再采用相对地道的目标语,尽量将原诗中那些言外之意的真情实感充分传达出来。这样一来,目标读者才有望读懂并理解诗句的意境,才不至于因为语码转化而曲解原文。由于青年诗人牛涛的诗歌创作总是饱含深情、满怀厚意,他写到动情处,每每欢呼雀跃并激动地流泪。在我看来,理解并与诗人牛涛保持某种同理心和情感共鸣度,则是英译其汉语现代诗的关键。只要能够准确地把握住诗人的这些真情实感,再运用目标语中最简单的词语和最简单的句子去呈现,去传译,对英汉两种语言得心应手地去编码、解码,翻译任务就算是完成了。至于许渊冲老先生所提倡的那种"音美、形美、意美"的"三美"诗歌英译,应该说是一种很难企及的目标。

当然,至于英译是否达到了瓦尔特·本雅明(Walter Benjamin,1892～1940)所说的那种"来生"(Afterlife)和"再生"(Reproduction)效果,那就仰仗读者去对照阅读,去自行体悟,并给予真诚的批评和指正了。正因为任何一种译文都是原作生命的延续,是原作的另一种"来生"。所以说,真正优质的翻译,必然要经历原著语言的更新和自身语言的降生。衷心希望读者能从我们的英译文稿中体会到本雅明式的"来生"感悟。需要强调的是,由于英汉两种语言存在着巨大差异,我们在英译过程中对"形合"和"意合"、"归化"和"异化"等翻译策略都作了灵活处理,每每"得意而忘形","求形而失意"。例如,英译中增补了"Cupid""Dionysian ecstasy""Heidegger""Holzwege""Strauss"等之类的西方文化专有词,希望这样的处理方式能够得到原诗作者和读者的理解和谅解。

令我欣慰的是,这本诗歌的英语翻译,时断时续,前后延续了差不多两年半的时间。其间得到了《香港散文诗》季刊主编、著名散文家钟子美先生的大力鼓励与支持,特此致谢。感谢河南大学出版社靳开川主任和张珊老师认真负责的专业奉献精神。衷心感谢本书责任编辑刘利晓女士耐心细致的反复审校,避免了很多尴尬的失误。感谢广州大学图书馆外语学科组组长姚艳萍女士精心周到的资料援助和文献查阅服务,使得本书的英语翻译变得高效便捷。感谢日本籍老师纯子小姐的热心支持。衷心感谢知名消化科专家、广东省道德模范徐克成教授和远在海外的藤原博士的关心、关注和指导,使得我们的翻译变得更有序、更有趣、更有益。感谢青年才俊牛海先生的长期合作和友情支持。他那份独有的人文情怀和精神守望,在当下浮躁迷惘的社会环境中显得弥足珍贵,令人感动和赞赏。感谢广州大学外国语学院研究生徐恒同学,作为本书译诗的第一读者,她总能给我的英译过程带来愉悦的阅读分享和贴心的译诗意见。

特别感谢《人民作家》公众号平台陈劲松主编的大力支持与提携。她热情地先行发表了本书的部分英语诗稿,让我从中可以征求读者的批评意见。感谢《人民作家》特约主播、志愿者高海燕,深圳大学博士研究生丁婕,《人民作家》平台特约主播张蕙芬女士声情并茂、情真意切的诗歌朗诵。

值得一提的是,书中所有插图都是由朋友圈的朋友和同事们提供,并经由译者铅绘素描处理,目的在于提高阅读乐趣,增加诗文内容和译文效果的直观性。所选的插图与诗文创作本身并无直接关联,特此说明。图片的使用如有冒犯之处,还请各位友人多多海涵,不胜感激。

陆道夫
2018 年 7 月 12 日初稿于杭州青山湖玫瑰园
2019 年 12 月 19 日修改于广州小谷围岛
2020 年元旦定稿于澳门何东图书馆